Melanie took a step toward the man with the silver eyes. "Excuse me for interrupting, but if you've only come here to insult our product, then you may as well stop wasting everyone's time and go away."

The man didn't seem to hear her. "Mel Stafford," Wyatt said genially. "I believe you're the manager."

"Yes, I am. And I'm asking you—no, I'm *telling* you—that it's time to go."

"But I'm not going anywhere," he said. "I'm your new boss."

Leigh Michaels has always been a writer, composing dreadful poetry when she was just four years old and dictating it to her long-suffering older sister. She started writing romance in her teens and burned six full manuscripts before submitting her work to a publisher. Now, with more than 70 novels to her credit, she also teaches romance writing seminars at universities, writers' conferences and on the Internet. Leigh loves to hear from readers. You may contact her at P.O. Box 935, Ottumwa, Iowa 52501, U.S.A., or visit her Web site: leigh@leighmichaels.com

Books by Leigh Michaels

HARLEQUIN ROMANCE®

3720—BRIDE BY DESIGN
3731—MAYBE MARRIED
3748—THE MARRIAGE MARKET
3759—THE BILLIONAIRE BID
3772—THE BRIDE ASSIGNMENT
3783—PART-TIME FIANCÉ

THE TAKEOVER BID
Leigh Michaels

TORONTO • NEW YORK • LONDON
AMSTERDAM • PARIS • SYDNEY • HAMBURG
STOCKHOLM • ATHENS • TOKYO • MILAN • MADRID
PRAGUE • WARSAW • BUDAPEST • AUCKLAND

ISBN 0-373-03800-3

THE TAKEOVER BID

First North American Publication 2004.

This edition published by arrangement with Harlequin Books S.A.

® and TM are trademarks of the publisher. Trademarks indicated with ® are registered in the United States Patent and Trademark Office, the Canadian Trade Marks Office and in other countries.

www.eHarlequin.com

Printed in U.S.A.

CHAPTER ONE

THE wind was strong, even for April, and the walls and roof of the metal building creaked a mild protest with every gust. Melanie knew perfectly well that it was not nearly as cold outside as it sounded. Still, she thought, the whine of the wind was enough to make Santa Claus shiver. As if in echo, the lop-eared dog at her feet whimpered in his sleep.

She heard the bang of the door between the shop and the office. Melanie turned away from the computer screen and glanced up at the big old-fashioned clock on the office wall as one of the workmen came in, wiping his hands on an already-greasy rag. The dog raised his head inquisitively and then, seeing the workman, put it back down on his front paws.

Melanie pushed her chair back. "I didn't know you were still here, Robbie."

"I stayed to put another coat of wax on Mr. Stover's Buick," he said. "It just didn't look quite shiny enough."

Melanie smiled. "I appreciate that you take care of the cars we work on as if you own them yourself. And he'll appreciate it when he picks it up tomorrow."

He shrugged. "We want the customer to be happy. When he's paying as much as Mr. Stover did to restore a '70 Buick, an extra coat of wax is nothing. Want to come and see it?"

She'd seen the car that afternoon. She'd seen it every day for the last month, as a matter of fact, watching every step of the restoration. But the gleam in Robbie's eyes and the note of pride in his voice told her it would be cruel not to go and admire his work.

She followed him back to the shop, the dog trailing behind. Robbie tossed the rag into a pile and picked up what looked like an equally-greasy one from a nearby bin.

"I'm never sure whether you guys are taking grease off your fingers or putting it on," Melanie said. Then she looked past him at the car sitting in the nearest bay of the shop, its baby blue paint and snowy white convertible top gleaming quietly under the harsh work lights. Souvenir of another age, it looked as long as an ocean liner by modern standards. "It's a beauty."

"Yeah." Robbie's voice was almost reverent. He brushed the back of his hand across the fender. "Quite a little different from when you found her sitting out in the back of the yard."

Melanie didn't have to think hard to remember what the Buick had looked like. "Buried under a pile of rusty fenders, with a mouse condo in the back seat and an engine that hadn't seen oil in twenty years—yes, it's a little different now."

"She runs like a dream. Want me to start her up?"

He'd love to have the excuse, Melanie knew. "Let's wait till morning and you can move it into the showroom so Mr. Stover will get the full effect."

The dog wheeled toward the door leading into the office, then bristled, growled, and started to bark.

Robbie frowned. "It's a little late for customers, and the door should be locked anyway."

"That'll be Jackson. He's got a key. Knock it off, Scruff." The dog stopped barking, but a soft growl lingered deep in his throat. Melanie pushed the door open and called, "I'm out in the shop."

A young man came out of her office, his camel-hair topcoat swinging open to reveal a black tuxedo. His white-blond hair was styled with such perfection that Melanie wondered how it was possible the wind hadn't ruffled it. Had he stopped to comb it the moment he came in, or was it actually sprayed into place?

He sounded almost grumpy. "I was beginning to think you'd forgotten and gone home."

"Oh, I couldn't forget your once-a-month visit any more than you would," Melanie said dryly.

Jackson's gaze fell on Robbie. "I'm not interrupting anything, am I?"

The tone of his voice obviously wasn't lost on Robbie, for his face turned red. "Want me to stay, Melanie?"

"No, Angie will be waiting for you." He went out, and Melanie said gently, "As a matter of fact, Jackson, you are interrupting. I was inspecting our latest project. Robbie just finished working on it." She walked slowly around the car, noting the finish on the chrome trim and the way light reflected from the paint. Robbie had been right about the effect of that last coat of wax. She'd have to remember to compliment him in the morning.

Jackson looked at the Buick. "Why anyone would pay good money for that..."

"That's the customer's choice, and don't expect me to believe that it bothers you to spend your share. You look very fine tonight, Jackson. And on a Thursday, too... Is it just dinner tonight, or the theater?"

Jackson raised his eyebrows in a well-practiced gesture. "It's never *just dinner* when you go to the Century Club."

Melanie wondered sometimes whether Jackson light-

ened his hair or darkened his eyebrows; the combination
was so improbable that she was sure it had to be one or
the other. "Of course. Well, you can't expect me to
know, since I've never been there."

"If you're hinting for an invitation, Mel—"

"Heavens, no. I wouldn't know what to do."

Jackson laughed. "Well, that's no doubt true. I'd love
to stay and chat, but Jennifer's waiting for me to pick
her up."

He hadn't needed to clarify that the no-doubt elegant
Jennifer wasn't waiting outside in his car, because he'd
never brought her to the shop. Melanie wondered sometimes if he'd ever told his most-recent girlfriend where
he got his money.

"So if you've got my check ready—"

"It's in my desk." She led the way, turning off the
shop lights as she went.

Jackson eyed the figures on the check. "Not much
this month. How do you live on this kind of money?"

"I don't," Melanie pointed out. "That's your share
of the profits of the partnership for the month. But in
addition to my share, I also draw a salary for working
here."

"That's not fair."

"Exactly what isn't fair about it? If we hired a manager, we'd pay him and then split what was left. I'm the
manager, so I get paid. If you don't like the bottom line,
you can start working for the business too."

"I do work for the business. I tell people about it all
the time."

"And in the last year, one of them actually turned up
to take a look. Of course, he didn't buy anything."

"That's not my fault. I tried."

"Well, maybe if you tried harder, you'd notice the results in your check. See you next month, Jackson."

Melanie locked the door behind him, shut down her computer, and called the dog, who was still standing pugnaciously by the entrance as if expecting Jackson to come back. "You won't have to defend me from him again for another thirty days, Scruff. Come on, let's go home."

She paused beside the back door and looked thoughtfully at the board where at least twenty tagged car keys were hanging from pegs. "What should we drive tonight, Scruff? It's too windy for a convertible, even with the top up. Do you feel like riding in a Corvette that's older than I am, or a Thunderbird that's only slightly younger?"

The Thunderbird was closer to the door, so that decided it. She grabbed the key and went out into the wind, still thinking about Jackson. He must have been in a hurry to get to Jennifer tonight, for he hadn't started in on Melanie as he usually did about wanting her to buy his share of the business.

Not that she wouldn't like to buy him out. In fact, she'd do it the very minute she found a spare half-million dollars lying around. Or whenever Jackson decided to be more reasonable about his price.

In Melanie's opinion, it was a toss-up which would happen first.

By the time Melanie arrived at the shop the next morning, Robbie had already moved the Buick. He hadn't put it into the showroom as she'd planned, however, but right outside the front door. He'd put the top down and parked the car at a rakish angle so the chrome caught the bright sunlight.

He was buffing the hood when she parked the Thunderbird nearby and strolled over. The dog hopped out of the car and began to make his usual morning rounds of the parking lot.

"Aren't you afraid it'll get a speck of dust on the windshield out here?" Melanie teased.

"I figured it would be good publicity." Robbie jerked a thumb toward the highway which ran along the front of the lot. "Traffic's been slowing down to take a look."

"I don't doubt it." She shaded her eyes with her hand and watched a pickup truck pull into the lot. "It's too bad we can't leave it here all week, but here comes Mr. Stover now."

She'd learned, in a couple of years in the classic car business, when to keep her mouth shut. So when Mr. Stover got out of the truck, she called, "Good morning," and then didn't say another word until he'd had a chance to look his fill.

That took a while—which was another thing that Melanie had learned from experience.

If it did nothing else, she'd found, being in the business of selling exotic, collectible, and antique cars taught patience. Patience with prospective buyers who wanted a specific model and color and wouldn't settle for anything else no matter how long it took to find. Patience with sellers who couldn't make up their minds whether to part with their treasures. Patience with the slow and painstaking pace of restoration work.

Of course, it was much more fun to be patient while Mr. Stover got his first look at a fully-restored, shiny-as-new Buick. If he wanted to stare at his new toy for an hour, Melanie would stand there quietly, leaning on a green Chevy, joining in his appreciation of a job well done, and waiting for him to break the silence.

From the corner of her eye, she saw a car pull off the highway and into the lot, and the shape of it rang bells in her brain. A Baritsa? She'd only ever seen one before, in person—but once noticed, the rakish lines and sporty silhouette were hard to forget.

She turned her head to look more closely at the car. It was a Baritsa, all right—a brand-new one, glossy black and showroom-shiny. Not at all the sort of thing that their regular clientele drove.

Maybe Jackson had taken her seriously. If he'd gone to the Century Club last night and started talking up classic cars to people who could afford fleets of them...

Don't get your hopes up. More likely it's someone looking for directions.

The Baritsa nosed in between the Chevy she was leaning on and a 1950s Packard with a "sold" sticker on the windshield. But the engine continued to purr.

Beyond the tinted window of the Baritsa Melanie could see only the shape of the driver's head and shoulders. A man, obviously. Probably tall, judging by the distance from the steering wheel up to the shadow that must be his chin. His hand was raised, as if he was holding a cell phone to his ear. But that was all she could tell.

Mr. Stover called her name, and Melanie jerked upright, wondering how long he'd been standing there in front of her while she gawked at the Baritsa. "Sorry," she said. "I didn't quite hear what you said."

"It's like a dream, you know." There was a catch in his voice. "I've always regretted selling my Buick, because it was the first car I ever owned. To get one just like it, and have it turn out so beautiful..." He smiled and reached into his pocket to pull out a checkbook. "I guess you're going to want some money, though—right?"

"Let's go inside to deal with the dirty work," Melanie suggested. She couldn't help looking back toward the Baritsa as she pushed herself away from the Chevy's fender.

Mr. Stover had obviously seen the Baritsa too. "I wonder what that guy wants. It looks sort of odd, him just sitting there like that."

"Maybe the Buick caught his eye and he wants to buy it from you."

"He can try," Mr. Stover said, and grinned.

Melanie ushered him into her office, handed him the car's papers, and went back to the showroom to get him a cup of coffee while he looked over the invoice.

The coffee machine was just finishing its cycle. She waited till it was done, poured two cups, and gathered up sugar and cream. The outside door opened, and she felt a flicker of excitement as she looked up. It was perfectly silly, of course, to get all breathless over a prospective customer, no matter what kind of car he drove. Still—a Baritsa...

But the man who came in was Jackson.

She could hardly believe her eyes. Jackson, dropping in on a Friday when he'd picked up his monthly check just the night before? Stopping by in daylight, when someone might actually see him there?

And since when did Jackson drive a Baritsa?

He probably borrowed it from Jennifer, she thought. *I wonder what she'd think about him using it to go slumming.*

"Mel," he said. "I need to talk to you."

"Not right now, Jackson. Customers first, you know—and I have one in my office waiting to write a check. A big check."

''It won't take long. I just need to tell you I've come for—''

She shook her head and walked past him, closing the office door firmly behind her.

Fifteen minutes later, she weighted Mr. Stover's check to her desk with a chunk of Missouri limestone and walked him through the showroom to the parking lot, watching with satisfaction as the Buick pulled out into traffic. The Baritsa was still there, she noted, but Jackson was nowhere to be seen.

As she went back inside, a muffled commotion from the shop drew her attention, and she walked across to open the door. ''What's going on out here? Is somebody hurt?''

''Not yet.'' Robbie sounded grim.

''Then what's all the ruckus?'' Melanie folded her arms across her chest and surveyed the group. Robbie, two of her other workmen, and Jackson had formed a sort of huddle in the empty bay where the Buick had sat till this morning. So this was where Jackson had gone.

Odd, she thought. He never went into the shop unless he had to, and then he'd hover by the door, obviously anxious not to touch anything—as if he was phobic about grease.

Robbie glared at Jackson. ''He's trying to steal a bunch of tools.''

''Steal!'' Jackson sputtered. ''That's slander! They were my father's tools, and now they're mine. I'm just taking what's mine.''

Melanie stepped forward. ''Wait a minute. Why do you even want them?''

''Good question,'' one of the workmen muttered. ''He wouldn't know what to do with them, that's for sure.''

''And in any case,'' Melanie went on, ''they weren't

your father's personal property, they belong to the business. Which you own half of anyway, so why you're making a fuss about tools—''

The shop door opened behind her and she turned to face the newcomer. ''I'll be right with—'' Her standard smile of greeting froze on her face.

The man in the doorway was tall and broad-shouldered, with midnight-black hair and eyes that looked almost silver when he pulled off his sunglasses. His features were too craggy to be considered hand-some—he'd be no competition for Jackson in a Greek-god contest. And yet there was something compelling about his face, something that wouldn't let her look away. Where Jackson was conventionally good-looking, this man was interesting. And in thirty years, when Jackson's good looks were long gone, this man would still be worth looking at…

Whoa, she told herself. She swallowed hard and started over. ''I'll be right with you.''

''I'll wait.'' His voice matched his eyes, smooth and polished as sterling silver. ''I'm in no hurry.''

''I'm sorry,'' Melanie said with genuine regret, ''but our insurance company doesn't allow customers to be in the shop area because of the potential for injuries. If you'll step back into the showroom for a moment—''

''I'm not a customer.''

Pieces clicked together in Melanie's mind. It wasn't Jackson who'd been driving the Baritsa, as she'd assumed. It was this man who had been behind the wheel.

Just my luck that he's not a customer.

His gaze had slid past her to the group of men. ''I'm looking for Mel Stafford.''

Melanie took a step forward. ''You found her.''

He looked startled. *''Her?''* He stared at Melanie.

That was another thing she'd gotten used to, Melanie reflected. People didn't expect a woman to be selling collectible cars. Keeping the books, maybe—but not running the business.

At least she'd thought she was used to that reaction—and there was certainly no reason to be irritated because this man had made the standard assumption. If he thought it would make a difference when it came to a deal, he'd find out soon enough that he was wrong.

But he's not a customer, Melanie reminded herself. *So what is he?* "What can I do for you, Mr.—?"

He didn't answer. His gaze was roaming over the building as if taking inventory of the eight bays, from the almost-finished Model T Ford right behind the group of workmen to the shell of a Mustang in the farthest corner.

"Jackson," he said, "I thought you told me this business deals in classic cars."

So maybe she hadn't been altogether wrong after all. Maybe Jackson had actually taken seriously what she'd said about promoting the business. Not that he seemed to have been very selective about who he talked to.

Jackson looked out from behind Robbie's shoulder. "Well, it does. Sort of."

"It's not what I'd call the Lamborghini capital of the world."

"I never said—"

"In fact, it looks more like a junkyard."

Melanie took a step toward the man with the silver eyes. "Excuse me for interrupting, but if you've only come here to insult our products, then you may as well stop wasting everyone's time and go away."

She heard Robbie gasp, and she had to admit that she was almost as surprised as he obviously was. She'd certainly never thrown out a customer before. Or a non-customer, for that matter.

The man didn't seem to hear her. "Mel Stafford," he said genially. "I believe you're the manager."

"Yes, I am. And I'm asking you—no, I'm *telling* you—that it's time to go."

"But I'm not going anywhere," he said. "I'm your new boss."

Wyatt had expected the news might come as a bit of a shock, because the moment he'd caught sight of Jackson—or more to the point, the instant Jackson had caught sight of him—he'd realized that Jackson hadn't yet shared the news with the employees. If he had, he wouldn't have ducked behind the nearest set of broad shoulders.

He's probably trying to pretend none of this is happening.

But Wyatt hadn't anticipated that his announcement would hit with the same concussion as a grenade. The three guys in grease-smeared coveralls looked as if he'd hit each of them right in the chin with a spade. Jackson turned an even more sickly shade of green and rubbed his index finger along the bridge of his nose. *Trying to hide behind his hand,* Wyatt thought.

And then the manager—what kind of a woman called herself *Mel,* for heaven's sake?—started to clap her hands together as if he were in the middle ring of a circus and had just pulled off an especially entertaining trick.

No, not at all the kind of reaction he'd anticipated.

She finally stopped applauding. "Nice try. As practical jokes go, that isn't a bad one. I don't quite know why Jackson would bother to set us up, but we've all certainly gotten his money's worth from the stunt. Now if you'll let us go back to work—''

Wyatt moved a little closer. "This is no practical joke, Mel.''

Her eyes were green, he noted. At least the part of them that wasn't shooting sparks at him looked green. A green-eyed redhead—now there was a dangerous combination.

"That's *Ms. Stafford* to you, Bub.''

"All right, Ms. Stafford. If this is a practical joke, why is my good buddy Jackson standing over there looking the color of mashed peas, instead of laughing?''

She wheeled around to stare at Jackson, and Wyatt watched with satisfaction as reality hit her. "What the hell have you done?'' she breathed.

Jackson seemed to shrivel.

Interesting phenomenon, Wyatt thought. *That's the first change we'll be making, because I can't have a manager who thinks she can order the boss around.*

He watched emotions chase each other across her face. Incredulity was followed by horror, which gave way to a sort of resigned shock. She blinked and finally noticed the gaggle of workmen who were watching, mouths agape.

"Robbie, get your crew to work,'' she said crisply. "Mr. Barnett will be expecting his Model T to be finished this week. Gentlemen, if you'll step into my office, the three of us will discuss this.''

"Mel, I—'' Jackson was almost whimpering.

Wyatt took pity on him. "There's no need for Jackson to be involved. He and I arranged the matter of ownership between ourselves last night. So it's only you and I who need to take up the details—Ms. Stafford.''

Jackson appeared too pathetically grateful even to

speak. He slithered past the workmen and out the side door before Mel Stafford could even react. Then she glared at Wyatt as intently as a vulture who'd been robbed of her prey. "You'll regret letting him go," she announced.

"We'll see." Wyatt stood aside to let her lead the way.

As he followed her across the shop and into the showroom, he noticed the crisp button-down Oxford tucked neatly into the waistband of her trim, well-worn jeans. And he wondered if the decided wiggle to her hips was an offshoot of being mad or if it was just a natural part of her walk. Not that he would have time to find out, for Ms. Stafford wasn't going to be around for long.

She led the way to the one small office which opened off the showroom and sat down firmly behind the cluttered desk. Wyatt decided not to squabble over who had a better right to the boss's chair. She was still the manager, after all. For the moment.

From under the desk a shaggy head protruded, and a long nose sniffed noisily at Wyatt's ankles. It looked like a mop with ears.

"Down, Scruff," Mel Stafford said firmly, and the mop retreated.

Wyatt lounged into the seat across from her, planted his elbows on the wooden arms of the chair, tented his fingers under his chin, and waited.

She moved a chunk of stone out of the way. "I gather, from what you said out there, that you think you've bought Jackson out."

I think I've bought him out? You wish I was only thinking, lady. But he had nothing to lose but a little time. Let her talk. Let her fool herself, if she wanted.

Let her think she's in charge.

Of course, it was none of her business how the change of ownership had happened. "In a manner of speaking," he said.

She nodded. "Do you know him well?"

What was with the sudden chattiness? He might as well warn her that a feeble effort at charm wasn't going to get her anywhere. Not after the fireworks she'd already displayed. But why make it easy on her? It might be amusing to watch her attempt to beguile. "A few months, I suppose."

"I see. How much did you pay him?"

Wyatt lifted his eyebrows. "I don't see why that would be any of your business, Ms. Stafford."

"Oh, I assure you it isn't just idle curiosity—though I must admit to feeling some. The last time he mentioned a figure to me, he wanted half a million dollars."

"That's very interesting. You sound as if you think your…um…car business isn't worth that much."

She smiled.

Wyatt could smell danger. She looked as if she was having a good time. This was not going quite as he'd planned.

"No, I don't," she said. "In fact, I think that price is pretty steep—for his half."

Half? The bonehead had never bothered to mention that he only owned half of the business. *And that surprises you, Reynolds?*

Or was it Mel Stafford who was pulling a con, trying to convince Wyatt to give up and go away?

He must have looked suspicious, but she drew herself up squarely. "I have all the paperwork to prove that Jackson's a half owner."

Now he was really leery. "Right. It's here somewhere. And I'm sure you'll be happy to dig it out and show it to me someday—when you have enough time. Probably around the turn of the next century. Come on, Ms. Stafford, stop trying to run a bluff on me.''

''I assure you, it's no bluff. Jackson's father was a small-town mechanic. How he ended up owning half a junkyard, I'm not quite sure—''

Wyatt didn't think his expression had changed an iota, but she paused and looked at him thoughtfully.

''Oh, yes,'' she admitted, ''your assessment was quite right. It does resemble a junkyard, because it used to be one. It's only in the last couple of years that it's taken on a new role.''

''And become some kind of gold mine.''

She frowned. ''More like opals, I'd say. We shovel tons and tons of debris to find one small jewel.''

The woman sounded absolutely serious. But she couldn't be for real. Could she?

''At any rate,'' she went on, ''Jackson's father ran the junkyard for years, stripping and selling parts now and then, but mostly just piling up more and more odd bits of vehicles. Where he got them all, I have no idea. When he died a couple of years ago and Jackson inherited, he wasn't too wild about the idea of being a junk man, so he immediately started talking about selling out.''

''For half a million dollars.''

''That was the price he named, yes. Of course, nobody's been crazy enough to actually pay him that much.'' Her eyes were very wide, very innocent, very green. ''Until now.''

And for your information, lady, nobody's been that crazy yet. But if she hoped a fishing expedition was going to get her the information she wanted, she'd have to improve the caliber of the bait, because Wyatt wasn't biting. "So if Jackson's dear old dad only owned half, who had the rest?"

"My father," she said. "Who left his share to me."

Wyatt knew he should have seen it coming. He should have known from the very beginning that getting involved with Jackson was like playing chicken with a diesel locomotive—somebody was bound to get hurt. He just hadn't thought far enough ahead to realize it could be him who ended up pasted to the rails.

She looked up dreamily at the ceiling. "So now that you know the whole story, I'm sure you'll want to hunt up Jackson and bail out of your agreement. Remember? I did tell you that you'd regret letting him leave this morning."

"I'm not going to hunt him down." His voice felt as flat as it sounded.

"But—" He saw consternation flare in her eyes. "But since he didn't exactly tell you the whole story—"

"No, he didn't," Wyatt said grimly.

"Then that's fraud."

"Probably so."

"And that means the deal's off. If you didn't understand what you were buying, then he can't hold you to the agreement."

"Unfortunately," Wyatt said, "it wasn't that sort of agreement. So the bottom line, Ms. Stafford, is that you've got yourself a new partner."

For the first time since he'd walked into the office, he felt the stir of satisfaction—because Mel Stafford's face looked even greener than Jackson's had.

CHAPTER TWO

PARTNER?

For a few seconds, Melanie was afraid she'd forgotten how to breathe—because when she tried it was like inhaling icicles. *Take it slowly,* she told herself. *A little bit of air at a time.*

The entire situation was perfectly clear—at least to her—and the appropriate response was obvious. But apparently the man sitting across the desk from her didn't see it the same way, or he wouldn't have blithely announced that he was going to be her new partner.

How on earth, she wondered, could anyone have actually agreed to buy a business without realizing that he was purchasing only half of it? Without checking things like a balance sheet or a profit-and-loss statement?

And even if for some incredible reason the deal had gotten that far, then why hadn't he gone storming out of the office to find Jackson and get his money back the instant he'd found out that he'd been taken for a ride?

Melanie had been absolutely certain of her ground. As soon as the Baritsa man had announced that he was the new boss, she'd known exactly what had happened. What *must* have happened.

So all she had to do, she'd thought, was to straighten out this flaw in his thinking. Once she had corrected his mistaken impression that he'd bought the entire business, the rest would take care of itself.

Or, rather, he would take care of it. Exactly how he chose to clear up the mess was none of her business. If he chose to settle matters with Jackson by beating him to a pulp, that would be too bad for Jackson, of course. But if Jackson was idiot enough to mislead a prospective buyer, he deserved whatever he got. It wasn't up to Melanie to interfere.

But now it seemed that the prospective buyer wasn't even going to try to straighten out the mess.

It wasn't that sort of agreement, he'd said. *You've got a new partner.*

Which made no sense at all. Why would he sit still for being taken like that?

Of course, it was becoming increasingly clear to Melanie that Jackson hadn't been the only fool involved in the deal. Agreeing to buy a business without even knowing for sure what kind of merchandise it carried, without looking over the stock, without checking out the bottom line to be certain the seller was telling the truth—

"That's the sort of thing my father would have done," she muttered.

"Pardon me?"

"Nothing." But at last a little light had dawned in Melanie's head.

Nobody would make a deal like that, blindly and without investigation, if he thought there was a chance he was being cheated. But the only kind of person who wouldn't have a healthy dose of skepticism over an offer of that sort was one who thought he was getting a sure thing. Or maybe one who'd been doing a little double-dealing of his own.

If he had believed he was the one doing the cheating, he wouldn't have been on guard against Jackson.

She doubted the Baritsa man would put it quite that clearly, of course. But it was the only thing she could think of which accounted for everything—including his unwillingness to go after Jackson now. *It wasn't that sort of agreement...*

"Do you have a name?" she asked abruptly.

"Oh, you can just keep calling me Bub. *Bub and Mel's Used Cars*—it has a certain ring to it."

Maybe he was delusional, Melanie thought wildly, and none of it had happened at all. "I don't suppose you have proof of this transaction."

His eyebrows lifted inquisitively, and Melanie couldn't help noticing that they had a natural aristocratic arch that was very unlike the practiced curve of Jackson's brows. "After watching your former partner ooze out of here on a wave of guilt that would fill a swimming pool, you still think you need proof that his share of the business changed hands last night?"

She couldn't argue with his point. How could she have forgotten for an instant the pathetic way that Jackson had crept out of the shop, refusing even to look at her?

No, there was no question the two men had agreed to some kind of a deal. The question was what she was going to be able to do about it.

Play along, she told herself. *Don't agree to anything. Just get him out of here and then you can call a lawyer and find out where you stand.*

He pushed himself up from his chair and started to look around the office. "You have a very interesting philosophy of decorating, Ms. Stafford. Why take down expired calendars when you can just hang this year's at the end of the row? Of course, eventually you'll run out of wall space. May I call you Mel, now that we're partners?"

"No," she said, a little more sharply than she intended. "I mean, I prefer to use my full name. It's Melanie."

"Interesting."

She was puzzled. "My name? I'm glad you think so, but—"

"I mean the idea that Jackson would ignore your wishes about your name as well as the business. At least I assume you don't approve of him selling his half."

"Perceptive, aren't you?"

"The question is why. I can think of several possibilities."

The phone rang. She put a hand on it and looked up at him. "Hold it right there till I finish with this call. I don't want to miss a word of your logic."

The caller was a regular customer, looking for a part for a car he was restoring. She put the phone down and reached for the intercom. "Robbie, when Fred has time, ask him to pull the driver's side door off the blue Mustang that's sitting out by the back fence. Bill Myers wants to pick it up this afternoon."

Robbie's voice came back, tinny and distant. "Sure thing."

She released the intercom button. "Now—you were saying?"

"Do you know every piece you have in inventory by heart?"

"Of course not. There's a whole corner of the junkyard we've hardly gotten into yet. But don't let me distract you from figuring out why I don't want Jackson to sell."

He held up a hand and began to tick off points on his fingertips. "You like having him around and wanted him to keep his share so you'd see him regularly."

"Don't make me laugh."

"Really? Then if you weren't gung-ho about having Jackson as a partner, what's so bad about him selling out?"

Melanie opened her mouth and closed it again. He had something there, she realized. Jackson had been a liability as a partner, a constant drag on the business. His unwillingness to reinvest any of his share of the profits had slowed the growth of Classical Cars, preventing Melanie from taking advantage of opportunities on more occasions than she could count. But since she couldn't do anything about Jackson's attitude, she'd concentrated on the things that she could control.

Now that he was gone, however…things were certainly going to be different.

"Another possibility," he went on, "is that you wanted to buy his half yourself."

"Not especially."

"But the two of you must have talked about it, because you had a figure in mind."

"Lucky you," Melanie said dryly, "to get there first and beat me out."

"I could be persuaded to sell, you know."

"I just bet you could—Bub."

"Wyatt Reynolds," he said, almost absently. "In fact, I'd like to sell."

"No fooling. And I'm sure all you want out of the deal is a teeny-weeny little bit more than you paid."

"I am a businessman, Melanie."

"If you say so—though if you regularly go around buying things sight unseen, I have my doubts about your judgment. Of course," she conceded, "even a few thousand would be a tidy little profit, considering you've owned it for just about twelve hours. I wonder what the interest rate would add up to on that investment."

"Would you care to talk about a price?"

Melanie looked him over thoughtfully. "Only if you'd be willing to buy my half at the price you're asking for yours."

"No, thanks."

"That's what I thought." Something was nagging at the back of Melanie's mind. "Reynolds— Do you mean as in the Reynolds family?"

"That was my father's name, yes," he said dryly.

"You know perfectly well I'm talking about the Reynolds family that started off with a mill on the banks of the Missouri River, selling flour to pioneers heading west in covered wagons, and ended up with a wheat empire that stretched all the way across Kansas."

"You know your local history."

"Seriously? You're part of that family tree?"

"A twig," he admitted.

"A good-size twig if you can afford to go around buying things without paying any attention to what you're getting. So what's the problem? You thought you'd bought the whole business last night. Why not finish the job and buy my half now?"

"You seriously want to sell it?"

Melanie started to nod, and then paused. Did she want to sell out?

It wasn't as if it had been her childhood dream to be in the old-car business. It had just happened, almost accidentally. She'd taken the lemon that life had handed her and tried not to dwell on the fact that she'd never liked the taste of lemonade.

But now that the possibility of getting out of the business was actually dangling over her head, she was hesitating, and she didn't know why.

It wasn't because she loved her job—though she had

to admit she didn't hate it anymore, either. At first, she had had to square her shoulders and grit her teeth every morning, and push herself with physical labor through the day so she'd be tired enough to sleep at night. But as the months and then the years went by, a weed-infested old junkyard had morphed into a moderately-successful broker of classic cars. And somewhere along the line, Melanie must have changed, too, or she'd be leaping at the bait Wyatt Reynolds was dangling.

Was she hesitating because she'd gotten to like the challenges of being in business? Or because selling would be like saying a final farewell to her father…? No, she wouldn't think about that.

More likely, she thought, it was because habit and inertia suggested that staying in a job she'd grown used to was less risky than venturing out into the world to chase a wild dream. But if the price was good enough…

"How much are you offering?" she countered.

"I'm not."

Melanie was annoyed that she'd let herself consider the possibility, even briefly. There was nothing to be gained by yearning over aspirations which were long gone. "Then what's the point in having this conversation?" She glanced at the old-fashioned clock mounted high on the wall. "I have work to do, Wyatt. I'll see you in a month."

He frowned. "A month?"

"To settle up," she said impatiently. "Jackson and I have—had—a pretty straightforward agreement. Once a month, I pay the bills and write the employees' checks. Then I take whatever's left and split it, half to each owner. Since he just picked up his check last night, the next one's not due for thirty days."

Wyatt was looking at her as if she'd snatched his brand-new wad of bubble gum.

"I see he also didn't tell you that he'd already collected this month's dividend." Melanie shook her head, feigning sadness. "You really don't know Jackson as well as you thought, do you?" The phone rang again and she reached for it. "When you leave, close the door behind you, please."

It was past noon when Melanie came out of her office, looking for coffee and an aspirin. She had to squeeze past the jutting tail-fin of a red Cadillac, and she wondered how on earth Robbie had managed to maneuver the car into a showroom that was approximately six inches wider than the car itself was. She was mildly relieved that she hadn't been there to watch.

The coffeepot was gone. The machine was still there, but the carafe to hold the brewed coffee had disappeared.

She growled and headed for the shop to raid the first-aid kit and the soda machine. But when she opened the door between showroom and shop, the mingled scents of engine exhaust, motor oil, and pepperoni almost knocked her over.

Three bays down, Robbie's guys had spread pizza boxes across the hood of an old Nash and pulled up stools, ladders, and odd parts to serve as chairs. Robbie's guys—and Wyatt. He was sitting atop a barrel which had once held clean rags, pouring coffee from the missing carafe.

"What are you doing out here?" Melanie demanded.

"Having lunch," Wyatt said. "We'd have invited you, but you said you didn't want to be disturbed."

"You know perfectly well I'm not asking about the pizza. Why are you still here?"

"I'm getting acquainted with the employees. Finding out about the business. Waiting for your lawyer to call back and tell you that you can't throw me out or void Jackson's deal."

"How did you—" She stopped herself, but it took a mighty effort.

"So you did try," Wyatt said.

Melanie decided not to dignify that with a comment. "I said I'd see you next month."

"That may have been the agreement you had with Jackson, but I don't happen to be the silent partner type."

"I'm getting the picture."

Robbie cleared his throat. "Time to get back to work, guys."

"Oh, don't let me interrupt the male bonding process." Melanie opened the wall-mounted first-aid kit and tore open a packet of aspirin. "If you can spare a cup of coffee, though…"

Wyatt filled a paper cup and handed it to her.

Melanie stared doubtfully at the cup. "You're sure this is coffee? It looks like ink." She took a tentative sip and winced.

"If that's all you're having for lunch, no wonder you're so hard to deal with."

"I am not hard to deal—"

"Let's talk about it in private." Wyatt picked up one of the cardboard rounds from a pizza box and chose three slices from the various leftovers.

One of the guys whispered to another, "A buck says he talks her around."

Robbie glared at him. "No betting on the premises, Karl."

Melanie led the way back to the office. Scruff sat up

in his basket and begged, and Wyatt pulled a scrap of ground beef off the pizza and tossed it to him. He set the makeshift plate on her blotter and perched on the corner of the desk.

Melanie walked around behind it and claimed her chair. She'd better, she figured, or he'd have his name engraved in the back before sundown. "I'm amazed you're still here. Surely you have other interests which require your attention."

"Not today. Now that you've had some time to think about it, Melanie…"

"What's to think about? It appears I'm stuck with you." She sat down. "You're right about the attorney, by the way. He read me a lecture about not getting a partnership contract drawn up a long time ago, but since Jackson and I have never agreed to any specifics about how to split up the business, he's perfectly free to sell his half to the first chump who comes along. Sorry—I meant, he's free to sell it to anybody he chooses."

"Thank you for telling me that."

"Why?" Melanie asked dryly. "Because it saved you the trouble of paying your own lawyer?"

"You could have strung me along."

"Would it have done me any good to try?" She picked a piece of pepperoni off the pizza and munched it absently.

"None at all. But your being honest makes things a little easier. Look, Melanie, this is the way it shapes up. You don't want me as a partner, but you can't afford to buy me out."

"That's about the size of it. And you don't want *me* as a partner—"

"And I don't want to buy you out. Which leaves both of us in a pickle."

She fiddled with a strand of cheese. "Are you summarizing for the fun of wallowing in pain, or do you have a plan for what we can do about it?"

Wyatt looked down at her, his eyes almost hooded. "We look for another buyer—and sell the whole thing."

"Easier to say than to do. Have you got any idea how long Jackson's been trying to sell out? Besides, I never told you I wanted to sell."

"Not in so many words, no," he agreed. "And of course I can't force you to. But the alternative is that you keep your share and I look for a buyer for my half."

Melanie shrugged. "Go ahead. I don't see that I'd be any worse off."

"Are you certain of that? You just pointed out yourself that without a signed agreement on how to handle a breakup, there's nothing preventing me from selling it to the first—how did you put it? Oh, yes—the first chump who comes along."

Melanie shook her head. "Nobody's going to buy it unless they're interested in old cars. Well, it's true you did, but even you have to admit you're not the average guy running around acquiring businesses."

"I wondered if you'd think of that. Your next partner might actually be the hands-on type."

"And even more trouble to have around than you are? That's hard to believe." He was right, however, and Melanie knew it. She'd thought Jackson was the world's worst partner because he hadn't been involved in the business. Now she was feeling nostalgic for the good old days. "Anyway, your chump will need to have half a million dollars to spend, too. The combination cuts the field down quite remarkably, I'd say."

"I never told you what I paid for my share. And I never said what I'd sell it for."

Melanie bit her lip.

"If I don't find a buyer soon," Wyatt went on, "I might even cut my losses entirely and give my share to the state prison system."

She couldn't stop herself. *"What?"*

He shrugged. "It's a natural. Some of those guys are already experienced at stripping cars down for parts. Of course they'd have to get used to the idea of buying the cars first, but I feel sure that you—as their partner—could persuade them to adjust."

She shivered. Which was silly, of course—he was only goading her to make his point.

At least, she hoped that was all he was doing.

Suddenly the room seemed stifling. She pushed back her chair, and Scruffy sat up in his basket and whined softly, the way he always did when he needed to go out. *Good old Scruff comes through again.* "I'm going to go walk the dog," she said.

"Great," Wyatt said genially. "You think about it and let me know. I'll be right here, getting up to speed on the business end of things. Which file drawer do you keep your records in?"

The bottom line was better than Wyatt had expected, though of course it was nothing which would excite a tycoon. And the cash flow was respectable, though there were times when the checkbook reflected a bank balance so low it would have kept Rip van Winkle awake at night.

He wondered if Melanie tossed and turned sometimes, worried about the business. He was dead certain Jackson hadn't.

The books were neat and clear and precise. Every part she'd ever sold—to a walk-in customer or at auction on the Internet—was documented. Every car that she had handled had its own code and its own file. Every piece which had been added to it and every hour's work were annotated, and with a glance Wyatt could tell precisely how much each job had cost and how much it had brought in. She didn't make a lot on any given car, but as far as he could see, she'd had only a couple that had been unprofitable. And they'd been early on—she learned from her mistakes.

But she hadn't been stretching the truth when she'd said she couldn't afford to buy him out. The wonder was that she'd managed to keep going, and keep growing the business, even with Jackson pulling his share of the profits out month after month.

Wyatt found himself puzzling not over the books, but the bookkeeper. The records she kept looked like a labor of love. They were meticulous, painstakingly complete. Yet when he'd asked if she wanted to sell, Wyatt had thought for a minute that she was going to leap at the chance.

He slapped the ledger closed. It was none of his concern whether she wanted to sell or not. And it was even more certain that he didn't care why.

He figured there were only three things she could do: Be sensible enough to throw in with him and sell the whole thing. Or be halfway sensible and not get in his way while he sold his share. Or lose her mind entirely and try to sabotage the sale.

It would be interesting to see which way she jumped.

He put the books away, glanced at his Rolex, and went out to the showroom to get another cup of coffee. Where had Melanie disappeared to, anyway? Was she walking the dog all the way to Oklahoma?

He inched his way around the end of the Cadillac and

stopped dead. A woman was standing near the door to the parking lot, her back turned to the room as if she was uncertain whether to stay or leave. She was young, she was very blond, and she was dressed in the tightest black leather pants he'd ever seen.

We need a buzzer on that door, he thought.

The woman's head was tipped to one side as she surveyed the bulletin board between the entrance and the office. It was full of photos of twenty, thirty, and forty-year-old cars, tacked up almost at random, and she was looking at the board as if she didn't believe what she was seeing.

She glanced over her shoulder and said, "It's about time someone showed up."

Lucky me. "I beg your pardon, but I didn't hear you come in."

She turned around then, her eyes wide as she soaked in the sight of him. "Do you work here?" She sounded astonished.

Wyatt stifled a sigh. "Not exactly. But I'll try to help."

She smiled and tossed her long hair. "I was looking for Melanie Stafford—but believe me, you'll do nicely instead. I'm Erika Winchester." She held out her hand.

"Wyatt Reynolds. Melanie will be back soon. She's just out walking her mop. I mean, her dog."

"I see." Erika's eyes narrowed. "*The* Wyatt Reynolds?"

A movement outside the front window caught Wyatt's eye. "Here comes Melanie now. That's a piece of luck." *Especially for me.*

The door burst open and Melanie came in on a swirl of wind. Her hair had come down out of its bun and was curling exuberantly around her shoulders. Her cheeks were pink, as was the tip of her nose, and her eyes were bright. She bent to release the dog's leash. "I hope you're not going to tell me that the black Mercedes out front is now a part of the inventory, because—" She stood up, caught sight of the woman, and broke off. "Erika?" She sounded almost as if the name had been forced out of her.

With obvious reluctance, Erika took her gaze off Wyatt. "Hello, Melanie. It's been a long time."

"A while, yes. What brings you all the way out here?"

Erika wrinkled her nose. "Now that you mention it, you *are* rather in the sticks, aren't you? I had no idea there were still little twisty highways like this one anywhere near Kansas City."

"Oh, we have all sorts of hidden treasures on this side of town."

Erika's gaze drifted back to the bulletin board, and then slid on to the Cadillac. "Whatever happened to all of your plans? The alumni office told me you were in the used-car business, but I didn't realize they meant such *very* used cars."

The rest of Melanie's face went as pink as her wind-reddened cheeks. Wyatt couldn't help seeing it. Unfortunately, he noted, Erika hadn't missed it either. Her eyes widened just a little.

And they say women are the gentle sex. "It's more like recycling," Wyatt said gravely. "You see—"

Melanie wheeled around to face him. "Thanks, Wyatt. But I don't think we need an explanation right now."

I was only trying to help, he wanted to say. But it was fine with him if she didn't want a hand. She was probably right anyway. *Reynolds, you have got to stop letting your Don Quixote impulses get the best of you.*

"So what can I do for you, Erika? Obviously you're not shopping for a car, if you're driving that black Mercedes."

Erika laughed. "No, of course not. Actually I'm not at all sure…" She started over with determination in her tone. "I'm working with the girls in the sorority house this year. Their project is raising money for the victims of domestic violence, and they've set up a charity auction for next week."

"So you're asking for donations?"

"Yes. Merchandise, services, vacation packages—of course, I thought of you and I knew if there was any way you could help, you would. It is your old sorority too, after all, even if you were only there for a couple of years." She turned back to Wyatt. "Tell me, is Melanie still a grind like she was in college? Always with her nose in the books. Biology and chemistry and…" She shivered. "Of course the rest of us all appreciated her, because she singlehandedly pulled up the house grade point average."

Interesting, Wyatt thought.

Erika looked around again, and put a hand out tentatively to brush the fender of the Cadillac as if wondering whether it could be real. "Honestly, it feels like a time warp in here."

"Thank you," Melanie said gently. "That's what we try to do—make every car look and drive as well as when it was brand-new."

Erika looked puzzled, then she shook her head and smiled. "Right. Anyway, that's why we're asking for donations. Though I'm not quite sure if you have anything… Well, perhaps you'll think of an idea."

The mop, who'd been sniffing the Cadillac's tires, stiffened and growled.

"Sit," Wyatt ordered him.

To his surprise, the dog sat.

"Well, I can't exactly donate a car without consulting my partner," Melanie said. "Let us talk about it and I'll get back to you. If you leave a number when I can reach you, Erika—"

Erika turned to stare at Wyatt. "Partner? You're a partner in this operation? You've actually got money in it?" She smiled. "No wonder you said you didn't exactly work here. I'm sorry. I'm sure it's not what it looks like, since you're involved, Wyatt."

Wyatt said, "I'm sure we could do something, partner—since it's for such a good cause."

Melanie glared at him. "And what do you have in mind—*partner?*"

"How about the Model T the guys are working on?"

Melanie gasped. "That's sold. You can't just give it away."

"How about giving it away for an evening?"

"If a musty old rattletrap is the best you can do—" Erika turned up her nose.

"I mean the use of a genuine antique car, restored to perfection, for an evening. If not the Model T, then perhaps this Cadillac." He patted the fender.

"Are you out of your mind?" Melanie's voice was low and almost hoarse. "Loaning out a car? I don't even let people test-drive these things without someone riding along. You can't take the chance of putting this car into the hands of a hot-rodder. It'll do a hundred and thirty on a straightaway—"

Wyatt cut across her. "A *chauffeured* antique car for an evening. And we'll throw in...let's say...dinner at Felicity's."

Melanie was sputtering. Between the red hair and the

sparks she was putting off, she looked like a firecracker that was about to explode.

"We'll get back to you with the details, Erika," Wyatt said. "But in the meantime—you can count on us for dinner for two at Felicity's, with chauffeur service."

Erika smiled at him. "Make it a really nice car," she murmured, "and I'll bid on the package myself."

She drifted out, and a couple of minutes later the Mercedes spun gravel in the parking lot.

Wyatt leaned against the Cadillac's fender, folded his arms across his chest, and waited.

"Well, it's obvious those leather pants of hers got to you," Melanie said.

"What? Oh, come on. It's a good cause."

"Maybe. But dinner at Felicity's? I thought you were going to look over the books. Surely you realize there is no money anywhere in the budget for dinner at Felicity's."

"I'll toss it in as my contribution to the cause."

"But why?"

"Just think of the attention it'll get when one of our cars pulls up in front of Felicity's. It'll cause quite a buzz. In fact, we should make a point of regularly getting the cars off the lot and out where they can be seen."

"I do," Melanie said. "I drive a different one every day."

"Where?" he asked shrewdly. "Back and forth to work? To the grocery store and the dry cleaner's?"

He'd got her, and it was clear that she knew it. "Not the dry cleaner's," she admitted, "because if a piece of clothing isn't washable, I don't buy it. Fine—it's your idea, you take care of it. Just think hard about which car you choose. Since Erika doesn't seem to be enthusiastic about vintage Cadillacs, you might try one of the Corvettes. Be careful, though—the transmissions can be tricky on those if you're not used to a stick shift.''

''Oh, I'm not going to be driving it.''

''I beg your pardon? I thought you understood I'm not about to loan—''

''Since you're so sensitive about who gets behind the wheel of your cars, and I'm the one who's providing dinner—''

He saw the instant she realized she'd been conned. ''Oh, no.''

''Then it's only fair that you be the chauffeur,'' Wyatt said gently. ''As you said yourself, we're partners. Right?''

CHAPTER THREE

HE'D boxed her in very neatly, Melanie had to admit. Though in a way she'd almost done it to herself, without much effort at all on Wyatt's part.

She'd had no intention of making a donation to Erika's cause, because she simply couldn't afford it. At least, she couldn't afford to give on the scale that Erika would find acceptable—and if Melanie offered anything less, Erika would probably have turned up her aristocratic little nose, refused, and then said something even more condescending than the remarks she'd already made. Melanie was still gritting her teeth over that crack about selling extremely-used cars.

Still, even if it had meant listening to Erika oozing false sympathy over Melanie's terrible financial condition, she should have just told the truth instead of dodging the question. Erika's fake pity would have lasted five minutes at the top end, and then she'd have stopped wasting her time with Melanie and moved on to the next potential donor.

But instead Melanie had made an excuse, and it was going to cost her dearly. *I have to consult my partner...*

She should have realized that acting as if Wyatt had a say in the matter would make him believe that he really did. Even so, she was still in shock at how he'd taken the idea and run with it—and then dragged her in, despite herself.

Chauffeuring someone around for a night on the town...what fun *that* was going to be. Especially if it

41

turned out to be Erika Winchester. Melanie wasn't going to whine about it, though, because that would only encourage him.

"You know," she said thoughtfully, "this could be a very interesting dilemma. If I'm driving, a Corvette won't be big enough because it only holds two passengers. However, Erika will want it to be just the two of you. So that means the Corvette would be perfect after all, except that you don't want to drive it, so we're back to needing a seat for the chauffeur.... I've got it. I'll teach you how to handle it, and then you and Erika can have a cozy—"

Wyatt shook his head. "I'm not sure I want to take driving lessons from someone who knows exactly how fast that Cadillac will go on a straightaway."

"Actually," Melanie said thoughtfully, "I don't know. Not firsthand."

"That's a relief. Who actually tried it out? Robbie, or one of the other guys?"

"I mean that I don't know precisely how fast it'll go, because I'm only guessing. The speedometer was buried and the car was still accelerating when I saw the curve coming and let off the gas."

"I hope you're going to tell me this was on a track and not a regular road."

"If it will make you feel better, I can tell you anything you want to hear."

Wyatt rolled his eyes.

"For heaven's sake, of course it was on a track. You don't think I'm idiot enough to drive that fast on a public highway, do you?"

"I don't think I should answer that," Wyatt murmured. "Anyway, let's worry about all the details when the time comes. Erika may not be the top bidder."

"You can hope. I suspect she'll not only win, but she'll want to spend part of the evening parked in a lovers' lane. Come to think of it, maybe the Corvette isn't such a good idea after all."

"Bucket seats," Wyatt mused. "Gearshift. I see what you mean."

"Definitely the Cadillac has more potential as a love nest. In the meantime, I have work to do." She eyed the narrow space between the car and the wall. Wyatt was occupying a good deal of it, and she would have to squeeze past him to get to the office. It would be easier to go around the car and climb through the back seat—except that would mean figuring out how to get the door open wide enough to get in. How had Robbie gotten out, anyway, with the car's convertible top up?

"If you're going to be hanging around here all the time," she added dryly, "I can find something better for you to do than polish that fender with the seat of your trousers."

He pushed himself away from the car. "I was just thinking about making a promotional tour."

"Good idea." She tried to stand aside to let him pass, but there was nowhere to go. As he slid by her, she felt the brush of his tweed jacket against her breasts. He paused, and Melanie had to restrain herself from climbing onto the hood of the Cadillac to get away.

How utterly foolish that impulse was, she told herself, because there had been nothing sensual about the contact. It certainly wasn't as if the man was incapable of controlling his impulses if he got too close to her. In fact, he'd probably laugh at the very idea of being overwhelmed by Melanie's sex appeal—especially with the image of Erika's black leather pants fresh in his mind.

Furthermore, Melanie wasn't attracted to him any more than he was to her.

But when the door closed behind him, she didn't go into the office. Instead, she opened the shop door and told Robbie to get the Titanic-size Cadillac out of the showroom immediately and bring in a car which would actually fit, with room left to walk around.

She told herself she was only doing it to show the merchandise in a better light and make it easier for the customers to get a good look.

It had nothing to do with Wyatt. Nothing at all.

Closing time passed, and Melanie locked the door. But an hour later she was still standing at the narrow counter which held the coffee machine, clearing up the last of the day's orders.

It had been busy all afternoon. Bill Myers had come as promised to pick up the replacement door for his Mustang, but instead of going home to work on the car, he'd planted himself beside her desk to chat for half an hour. The owner of the Model T which was nearing completion back in the shop had come to her to complain that the new upholstery wasn't quite the color he'd had in mind, and Melanie had had to talk him out of doing the interior in flame orange. And back in the shop, Karl had cut himself on the edge of a rusty fender and had to have three stitches and a tetanus shot.

Only during her walk with Scruffy had Melanie had a chance to think at all, and then her mind had been going in circles because of Wyatt's plan to sell the whole business.

She'd never given the possibility much thought before. As long as Jackson's share was drawing no nibbles, there had been no point in even thinking of selling her own. But Wyatt's conviction was contagious. If he was right, and they really could sell out…

The farther she'd walked, the more colorful her dreams had become. If the price was high enough, she wouldn't have to get another job. She could go back to school and follow through on the plans she'd made so long ago—the plans she'd had to put on the shelf when her father died. If only the price was high enough…

Then she'd come back to the shop. She had stood at the edge of the highway just outside the fence and looked at the makeshift metal building with its peeling paint and awkward lean-to additions. She'd looked at the row of cars out front, in various stages of restoration and repair. She'd looked beyond them to the still-weedy back half of the lot. And the grandiose dreams had burst like an overinflated bubble.

It was easy to dream when she wasn't looking directly at the facts. But once she was back on the lot, facing reality, it was impossible to fool herself. She didn't even have to dig out the ledgers; she knew the numbers almost by heart.

While the business was profitable, it wasn't such a stunning success that it could command top dollar from a buyer. Besides, she asked herself bluntly, who was going to want it?

It wasn't the sort of business anyone would buy as an investment, because there were easier ways to make a buck. Restoring old cars required large doses of labor, individual attention, and devotion to detail—not exactly the road map to high profits. So what were the odds of finding someone who not only had the money to finance the purchase but was fascinated with old cars as well?

Then there was the question of what Wyatt would consider to be a good price. Melanie was sure he'd want more than he'd paid—if he could get it. But how much was that? And even before he'd looked at the books, he'd as much as said that he wouldn't hesitate to cut his losses if he had to. What kind of penalty would he be willing to pay to get out of a bad situation?

It was an important question because the price he got would determine her cut as well. But if the payoff wasn't enough to fund her dream...

Then she would simply be trading this job for a different one. And if that was the case, she might as well stay right where she was. She knew she could make this work, because she'd done it for several years. And at least here she was her own boss.

She pulled a strip of tape off the roll and was slapping it onto a box when a key clicked in the door. Scruffy growled, but as Wyatt came in the dog gave one sharp yelp of greeting and bounced across the showroom toward him.

Melanie looked over the top of the little green roadster which had taken the Cadillac's place. "You again? I don't remember giving you a key."

"You didn't, Jackson did. Or perhaps I should say I insisted on getting it from him. Surely you wouldn't prefer that I'd have let him keep it so he could collect those tools at midnight when there's no one to stop him."

Melanie frowned. How had Wyatt known about the tools? She was certain he hadn't come into the shop that morning until after Jackson had made his stand. "Robbie must have told you about that."

"No reason he shouldn't tell me. They're half mine now. What are you doing?"

"Boxing up the radio from a 1964 Thunderbird to ship to California."

"California? How did the customer know you had it?"

"Have you ever heard of advertising, Wyatt?" She relented. "There's a bulletin board on the Internet for car restorers. People post what they want, or list what they've got for sale."

"Isn't that the kind of thing you could use yourself?"

"Not anytime soon. And considering what they're paying for this, I can't afford to hang on to it on the chance of needing it sometime in the future."

"What about the car it came out of?"

"Not restorable. It looks as if it hit a tree head-on, bounced off, and rolled. The radio's about the only thing that still works."

Wyatt pulled a stool from under the narrow counter and perched on it. "What do you do with the leftovers? If nothing but the radio works—"

"There's a place that buys scrap steel to recycle. Not that we make anything on it, but at least we get rid of the clutter that way. Hold this." She thrust the radio at him and padded the bottom of the box with foam.

"I walked around the lot this afternoon. There must be three acres full of cars and pieces out there, just sitting in the open to be rained on."

"It's more like five acres. What do you expect, anyway?" She felt a little irritable. "It would take a building the size of a football field to put it all under a roof. Probably several of them."

"What's the matter with you? I was only saying that—"

"Look, Wyatt, if you're going to spend your time around here, you need to get realistic, all right? It would cost the earth to protect every single part from snow and rust and rodents."

"I know," he said quietly. "I wasn't questioning your management."

Melanie bit her lip. It wasn't like her to be jumpy like this, and judgmental. "Sorry. I shouldn't have snapped at you. I'd like to have it all sorted and neatly arranged, but it would cost way too much to be practical. The shelving alone…" She set the radio into the box and added padding around the sides. "Anyway, what are you doing here? I thought you'd disappeared for the day."

"No, you thought you'd driven me off with that threat to put me to work. I could ask you the same question, you know. What are *you* doing here? Do you work all the time?"

"The phone rings all day, and customers want attention. So this is the only time I can concentrate on orders like this."

"Hire somebody."

"With what? The payroll's stretched as far as it will go. Unless you want the title of shipping clerk."

"I'd rather be in charge of sales."

"You have to earn that one. Get a few deals under your belt and then—"

"I don't mean selling cars. I mean selling the business."

Melanie folded in the top flaps of the box. "Hand me the tape dispenser, will you?" She didn't look at him. "Do you really think someone will buy it?"

"I don't see why not. There's bound to be interest."

"No, I mean sell it for enough money to…" She stopped, suddenly unwilling to admit how important the answer might be to her.

The silence drew out. "What is it you want to do, Melanie?"

She bit her lip. "Nothing."

"Literally nothing? Oh, no. I don't believe that you want to retire and sit in a rocking chair. Not at your age."

Melanie didn't answer. She hadn't shared her dream with anyone for so long—hadn't even let herself think about it—that now it felt just short of silly even to hope that it was still possible. Wyatt would probably laugh at the idea, and Melanie wouldn't blame him. Erika had certainly been amused by the fact that Melanie had ended up selling cars—and she'd known a lot more about Melanie's long-ago plans than Wyatt did.

"No," she said finally, "I don't want to be a couch potato. But I don't want to have to take another job I don't like, either."

"Another one?" Wyatt said softly.

She wished she hadn't let that slip. And yet, what difference did it make? If he believed she was passionate about this job, then he'd gotten the idea from someone besides her.

"How did you get stuck here, Melanie?"

"I thought I told you." The tape shrieked as she pulled a strip off the dispenser. "My father died, and someone had to take over."

"You didn't have any brothers who liked to tinker with engines?"

"No—there was just my mother and me. She died last year." She took a long breath and let it out. "So what's the plan for selling? I assume you have one?"

"We clean the place up while we're looking for a buyer."

She sighed. He wasn't saying anything she didn't already know. The entire yard looked tired and neglected—not exactly the way to a buyer's heart. But there were always a half-dozen places to spend each penny, and painting the trim on the building was well down the list.

"And beef up the business," Wyatt went on, "which means promoting."

"Wait a minute. If you have some big advertising campaign in mind—"

"As a matter of fact, I do—but not the kind that costs money. Erika gave me the idea."

"That would probably disappoint her," Melanie said under her breath.

"What do you mean?"

"Just that she'd rather have you thinking about her than about advertising."

Wyatt looked faintly interested. "You know, that's the second time you've warned me about Erika."

"And the last. A word to the wise, you know."

"Was she the kind who stole boyfriends in college?"

"Not from me."

Wyatt nodded thoughtfully.

Thanks for the tactful silence. But he might as well have come right out and said that Melanie couldn't possibly attract the kind of man Erika would be interested in. From the look on his face, it was absolutely clear to Melanie what he was thinking.

With a thump, she set the box atop the stack she'd already finished. She'd like to park it on his head.

"The charity auction idea caught my attention," Wyatt said. "Loaning a car for the evening is low-cost, and it potentially carries a big return."

"Or it might turn out to be a zero."

"Yes," he admitted. "But if nothing comes of it, we're only out a little time. So I was thinking, why stop there? If we get the cars out where they can be seen by the right people, we'll probably sell a few cars—but more importantly, we may also catch the attention of someone who wants the whole shooting match.''

Melanie shrugged. ''We don't have anything to lose by trying it, I guess. A tank of gas will go a long way.''

''And while we're doing that sort of promotion, we can be whipping this place into shape. Do we have to drop those boxes off somewhere?''

''No, the courier will pick them up tomorrow when he makes his regular deliveries.''

''Good. Because I think we should begin right now.''

''You mean tonight?''

''There's a new club opening up on the north side, and this week is their grand opening.''

Melanie stifled a yawn. ''Have a good time. There's a board full of keys by the back door. They're tagged so you know which car is—''

''Remember? I don't drive antiques.''

''Then you have a problem, because I didn't sign on to be your chauffeur.''

''How about being my companion? It's very dull going to a club alone.''

''Poor baby.'' She told herself it was silly to feel butterflies. The invitation had been issued only because she was convenient and handy, and it was about as far from being a date as she could imagine.

But of course the fluttering in her tummy definitely wasn't anticipation. It might be irritation. Aggravation. Maybe dread. But it certainly wasn't anything pleasant.

''I'd probably go to sleep during the first number,'' she muttered.

''Not at The Canteen Club. I hear it's the hottest place in town right now. Nostalgia's big, you know, and it's got some kind of big-band theme. Besides, you can start giving me driving lessons on the way.''

"I thought you'd given up the idea of a Corvette for your date with Erika."

"We need a backup plan, just in case we sell the Cadillac by then. I need you, Melanie."

The butterflies fluttered more strongly.

Wyatt said earnestly, "Because if anybody asks questions about the car, I wouldn't be able to answer them."

Well, that's a relief. I'd hate to think it was some personal need. "Oh, if that's the job you've assigned me," she said dryly, "I've got a better idea. I'll give you Robbie's phone number and you can take him instead."

Melanie hadn't seen him smile before—not a real smile—and she wasn't prepared. Wyatt's eyes crinkled just a little at the corners, and their silvery gleam warmed till it was like melted steel. There was a dimple at the corner of his mouth that made her want to reach out and touch it to be certain it was real. The overall effect was like focusing a bank of footlights on an ice cube, and almost instantly she found herself feeling a little warm and soft around the edges.

"I'm not dressed to go out," she said. But it was a feeble protest and she knew it.

"It's a casual club."

"What about the dog?"

"What do you usually do with him when you run errands? He can guard the car. Who knows, maybe we'll kick off a new fashion and people will want not only a classic car but a mop to match. We may even start a run on the animal pound. Come on, it'll be fun."

Melanie wasn't so sure of that, but she was dead certain he wasn't going to give up, so she whistled for Scruffy and went to get her jacket.

She looked carefully over the board full of keys and

offered Wyatt the one she finally selected. "Red Corvette, black interior. We haven't restored it yet, but it looks pretty good compared to most cars when we first start on them."

Wyatt shook his head and said solemnly that he felt he should observe for a while before he got behind the wheel of such a valuable piece of equipment.

Melanie shook her head in confusion. "I thought you didn't trust my driving because I raced the Cadillac."

He stopped halfway out the door. "You were *racing*? Not just running it on a track?"

"What's the point of driving that fast if you're not competing?"

"Hand over the key, Melanie."

"Wait a minute. What kind of a club did you say this is?"

"Nostalgia. Big band era."

"And it's called The Canteen Club? You mean like a world war soldiers' canteen?" She hung the key back on the board. "Then the Corvette would be anachronistic—what on earth was I thinking? We'll drive a 1940 Ford. A two-door with a flat-head V-8 engine."

Wyatt took a long breath.

"Relax, Wyatt. I didn't wreck the Caddy at a hundred and thirty, and I'm not going to tank the Ford either."

"That's a relief. I hadn't even thought to ask whether that little episode was the reason you had to rebuild the Cadillac."

"And the Ford won't do anything near that speed, anyway." She led the way across the yard. "Probably not over a hundred, in fact. Let's find out."

In the moonlight, she couldn't tell for certain whether Wyatt actually turned pale, but she felt a little better.

It was late enough that the freeway traffic was light,

but the Ford—chugging along precisely at the speed limit—got plenty of attention from the few other drivers on the road. A couple of them honked and waved, and a carload of teenage boys whistled.

Melanie waved back. "Maybe we should just drive around till midnight," she said hopefully. "More people will see the car that way than if it's parked in a lot somewhere."

"But you have to keep the audience in mind. Better one serious buyer than an entire busload of kids with no money."

"I suppose you're right. Wyatt... What about my guys?"

"You mean Robbie and the crew?"

"Yeah. What if they don't like the new owner? Or what if he lays them off?"

"If he's smart, he'll keep them."

"But what if he doesn't? Robbie's got a wife and a baby who's not a year old yet."

"Melanie, if you start putting conditions on a sale—"

"I know. Nobody wants to be told how to run their own business, and if they're paying for it, it's theirs." She sighed. "But I don't want my guys to be worried. There's no point in upsetting them about their jobs if nothing's likely to come of it."

"Now that's a defeatist attitude. You're assuming that no one will want to buy the business."

"That's not what I'm saying at all. You bought it, after all. I just want to wait to tell them till we know something definite."

Wyatt was frowning a little. "All right," he said finally. "If you feel that strongly about it, we don't have to tell them it's for sale till we know more. Here's the turn. The nightclub is that warehouse up ahead."

The building he pointed out didn't look like a night-club to Melanie. The building was big and mostly dark, though a couple of spotlights played back and forth across the facade, flickering on a sign which read The Canteen Club. The street was almost empty.

"I see there's no shortage of places to park," she muttered.

"The valet stand is right in front."

"Great. The parking valet will get a good look, but nobody else will. I told you we should stay on the free-way."

Wyatt smiled a little. "Are you always this grumpy late at night?"

"I'm fine. But now that you mention it, it *is* past Scruffy's bedtime."

"Then I'll definitely have to make it up to Scruffy." As soon as the car stopped, Wyatt got out and beckoned to the valet, who'd started around to Melanie's side of the car. She didn't hear their low-voiced conversation, but she couldn't miss the smooth movement of a couple of pieces of paper from Wyatt's hand to the valet's. Then the young man came around the car, opened Melanie's door, helped her out, and slid reverently behind the wheel. As she watched, the car backed up a few yards and turned slightly, and the engine died.

She took a step forward. "What happened?"

"He turned it off, Melanie."

"But that's a no-parking zone."

"Not tonight." Wyatt took her arm. "And everybody who comes in and out will see it sitting there."

Melanie hung back. "Are you sure you don't want to paint a sign on the windshield?"

"*'Buy me at Bub and Mel's Used Cars'*? How per-fectly crass."

"But what good will it do for people to see it if they don't know it's for sale?"

"The valet will take care of that. Trust me."

"How much did you pay him?"

"Enough," Wyatt murmured. "Now let's go have some fun and let the car work for a change."

CHAPTER FOUR

IT WASN'T the first time Melanie had encountered a doorman wearing a military-looking uniform, but she was startled to be greeted by a snappy salute—and when Wyatt returned it, she felt her eyes widen in surprise.

"Automatic reaction," he said, and tucked her hand into the bend of his arm. "I spent some time in military school when I was a kid."

She said sweetly, "I see. Was that where you acquired this tendency to order people around, or did you already have it before you went?"

"Actually," Wyatt said. "I got sent off to school because I'd pulled so many stunts no place else would take me."

He sounded perfectly serious, but there was a twinkle in his eyes. Melanie just wasn't sure whether it was because he was pulling her leg or fondly remembering his past.

There was a line of patrons in the lobby, waiting to be seated. Melanie peered around the large woman standing in front of them to get a first look at the decor. She couldn't see much except the maître d'. He wore a general's stars, and he was acting the part as well. Rather than seating people himself, he summoned assistants who were dressed in army green uniforms and matching caps, and barked out table numbers.

The system was efficient, Melanie had to admit—the line was moving along smoothly. They had nearly reached the general when a man came in from the street

57

and strode past the waiting crowd to the maître d's stand, ignoring grumbles from the patrons he had bypassed. His suit was cut with wide, padded shoulders and broad lapels, and he hadn't bothered to remove his snappy fedora when he came inside.

"George, there's a car parked out front," he said.

The general's air of authority slipped as if he'd just been addressed by the commander in chief. "Yes, sir. I'll have it towed immediately. And I'll find out which parking valet slipped up and fire him."

Melanie's fingers tightened on Wyatt's sleeve. "I told you we should have stayed on the freeway," she whispered. "Now you've cost that poor guy his job."

He patted her hand and drew her out of the line and toward the general.

The woman in front of them sniffed disdainfully as they passed. "Some people have no manners," she said loudly.

"So true, ma'am," Wyatt told her. "I've often despaired about that fact myself... Hello, Brad. Is the car a problem?"

The man in the fedora swung around. "Reynolds—good to see you. You mean that's *your* car out there stealing attention from my club? I thought you only drove Baritsas."

"That's true," Wyatt said. "Let me introduce you to the driver."

Great, Wyatt. Shift the blame onto me.

"Melanie, this is Brad Edwards. Brad—"

Melanie didn't wait for him to finish. She pulled the Ford's key from her jeans pocket and dangled it under his nose. "Mr. Edwards, I'll move the car right away. Please don't fire the parking valet. It wasn't his fault—"

"No, no," Brad Edwards said. "It's your car? Is it real?"

"—that Wyatt talked him into letting us park in..."

Wyatt's elbow bumped her rib cage, hard.

Melanie paused, distracted. "Did you ask if it was real? Of course it's—"

"Not some kind of faked-up replica?"

She bristled just a little. "No, it's the genuine article."

"And I bet she's got the paperwork to prove it," Wyatt said. "Why, Brad? Are you trying to buy it?"

"If the price is right," Brad said, "I might think about it. George, these people will be at my table." He swung around toward the main room without looking to see whether they were following.

"Better hold off on calling for a tow truck, George," Wyatt murmured. "The boss wouldn't like it if you hauled his car away." He tugged Melanie toward the door.

"Do you often have arm spasms like that?" Melanie muttered. "I'm going to have bruises where you hit me."

"*Nudged* you. Come on."

She couldn't help stopping in the entrance to take a closer look, however. The room looked like a cross between a ballroom and a YMCA. Along one side was a long counter which seemed to be part soda fountain, part bar. Opposite it was a huge stage, where a singer in blue taffeta was belting out a love song, backed by a big band that sounded heavy on the brass. Tables, nearly all of them full, surrounded the dance floor where a man in seaman's white was dancing with a woman in a sparkly pink gown.

"I am definitely underdressed," Melanie muttered.

Brad Edwards led the way to the last empty table near the bandstand, directly off the dance floor.

Wyatt followed her gaze to the dancers. "If you're talking about the admiral and his date, I'd bet they're part of the hired help."

Brad held Melanie's chair and grinned. "I don't usually admit it, but you're right, Reynolds. Their job is to provide a little encouragement to the regular folks to dance."

Melanie watched as the admiral and his partner executed a complicated spin. "*Very* little encouragement," she said. "If that's the expertise level you expect of your guests, I'll be sitting it out."

"While you're talking about a car," Wyatt reminded gently.

"How much do you want for it?" Brad asked.

Melanie drew a breath to tell him.

Wyatt stepped on her foot. "Let her think about it, Brad. Can she call you tomorrow, or do you want to call her?"

Melanie was exasperated. "Wyatt, I—"

"Sweetheart." His voice was like a caress. "You know how much that car means to you."

Yeah, she thought. *It represents a nice chunk of change—if we can shake hands on a deal before you mess it up.*

But before she could argue the point, Brad Edwards was pushing his chair back. He handed her a business card. "You can call me at this number tomorrow. And feel free to use the table the rest of the evening—I'll be circulating and greeting guests." He waved a uniformed waiter over and said, "Get these people what they want, Private."

The waiter pulled an order pad and pencil from his sock.

Melanie blinked in surprise.

He grinned. "It looks odd, I know, but it's the boss's orders—putting anything in the pockets ruins the lines of the uniform, and aprons just don't fit the image. What can I bring you?"

"I really don't— Oh, a white wine spritzer."

Wyatt ordered a scotch and soda.

Melanie held her tongue until the waiter was safely away from the table. "Thanks for killing the best opportunity I'll ever have to sell that car. Do you have any idea how long it's been sitting on the lot?"

"Since 1940?"

"I thought you wanted to promote the business."

"Melanie, you may know cars, but you don't know Brad Edwards. The longer he's denied something the more he wants it."

"Oh." She had to give him the point, because he obviously knew Brad better than she did.

"Besides, once he's had a chance to think over the idea, you may be able to sell him a package," Wyatt went on. "Maybe half a dozen cars. He could use them to ferry people around—provide a shuttle service for visitors who flew into town and don't have a car, or people who've had one too many drinks and need to be taken home."

"Nobody would put a drunk into an antique car. It would be too hard to clean the upholstery if he got sick, and too expensive to replace it."

"A vintage Jeep," Wyatt murmured. "No top, no windows. The passenger could just lean over the side."

"And they'd need to, because there's also no suspension and no springs. Have you ever ridden in one of those things?''

''I'd rather spend another year at military school.''

Melanie wasn't listening. ''What he really needs is a staff car.''

The private returned with their drinks.

Wyatt raised his glass and swirled his scotch and soda. ''Cheers. What do you mean, a staff car?''

''The kind that generals used, with a glassed-off compartment for the driver—separate from the back seat so the officers could discuss strategy without the driver hearing. Some of them were pretty plush.''

''Do you have one?''

''No—but I can start looking. Of course, a lot of them are in museums. Now that we've accomplished what we came for—''

''You mean by getting Brad interested? Why settle for one potential buyer when you could have several? Maybe you'll end up with a bidding war.''

She was watching the entrance. ''The place seems to be full, and I haven't seen anyone leaving.''

''We'll have to stay till the evening winds down and people start going home, to give them a chance to see the car. Let's order dinner. I promised the mop I'd make it worth his while to wait for us, so if I walk out without a doggie bag, he'll probably bite me.''

Melanie hadn't felt hungry until that moment, but she realized abruptly that she was famished. ''Scruffy growls now and then, but he's too well-trained to bite anyone.''

''I'll take your word for it.'' He waved the waiter over and asked for menus.

Melanie took one look and said, ''I have no idea what to order. There are no prices.''

"The general principle is that you order whatever you want to eat."

"And damn the expense? That's nice if you can afford it, but some of us are on a budget. And since I didn't get to the bank today to cash my paycheck—"

"Melanie, I'll buy your dinner. Have a T-bone steak and make the mop happy—that way he'll have two bones to chew on."

"I'll pay you back." She put the menu down, and he ordered for her.

"Let's dance," Wyatt said.

"I don't think so."

"Because you're not as good as the admiral?"

Because I don't want to forget that this isn't a date.

"Look at it this way," Wyatt said. "With the spotlights glaring off that white uniform, it's impossible to see what anybody else is doing on the dance floor. Polka, fox-trot, waltz, twist—it wouldn't make any difference what you did, because nobody would notice."

"I'll have to take your word for that, since the only one of those I can do is waltz. And I'm lousy at that."

"Come on. Give it a try." He pushed his chair back.

Reluctantly, Melanie stood up.

From the corner of her eye, she saw a young blond woman in a strapless red cocktail dress jump up from a nearby table and flounce toward them in as direct a path as was possible between the close-set tables. She sidestepped Melanie without a glance, raised her hand, and slapped Wyatt across the cheek.

To Melanie, the crack of the young woman's palm against his face cut across music and conversation alike, and she was surprised when the room didn't settle into a stunned silence. But apart from a few people at nearby tables, no one seemed to have noticed.

She stole a glance up at Wyatt, expecting him to show embarrassment, maybe even shame. But his face was perfectly calm. To Melanie's astonishment, he didn't even look surprised.

She doubted that he was accustomed to being slugged in public. But obviously he knew the blonde, so perhaps he'd anticipated that she might react violently when she saw him with another woman—no matter how innocent the occasion.

That must be it. He wasn't surprised, because he'd known how the blonde was likely to respond. And he wasn't embarrassed or shameful, because he'd done nothing wrong.

I wonder what she'd have done if this had really been a date.

He guided Melanie onto the dance floor. Figuring there had already been enough of a scene that a simple dance couldn't possibly make it worse, she didn't resist. She took a minute to catch the rhythm of the music, and then she said as casually as she could, ''Your wife, I presume?''

''Good lord, no.'' He sounded as if she'd knocked the breath out of him.

''Fiancée?''

''You're joking, right?''

''Not at all. *Former* fiancée?''

''Not even close. I thought you would recognize her.''

Melanie ran through her mental catalog of friends, acquaintances, and celebrities. To the best of her recollection, the blonde didn't fit into any of those categories. ''Should I have?''

Wyatt frowned. ''I'd have thought so. That's Jennifer.''

"Jennifer...." She was lost. "Jennifer.... You mean, Jackson's Jennifer?"

"That's the one. I wondered if she'd calmed down yet. Apparently not. You've been keeping a secret, Melanie."

Me? she thought in astonishment. *What about you?*

He swirled her around the floor and smiled down at her. "Lousy dancer, indeed. You're actually very good at waltzing."

By closing time, Wyatt was beginning to wish he'd put money into Brad Edwards's idea, because not only did The Canteen Club pack in the customers but it kept them there. Finally, however, the inevitable exodus began, and Wyatt said, "Are you ready to go?"

Melanie's eyes lighted up. "I've been ready for hours. I mean—" She hesitated and bit her lip. "Well, it's not like we were intending to have fun."

"It's all right," Wyatt said dryly. "Next time I'll try to find a form of entertainment that's more to your taste."

"Next time? If you're planning to make a habit of this, I'm not sure I can keep up." She tried, without much success, to stifle a yawn.

The air outside was crisp and cold, but despite a brisk wind, the Ford was surrounded by admirers. Inside, the mop quivered with indignation each time someone violated his personal space by touching the car. Wyatt opened the car door carefully so the dog couldn't get out, but Scruffy didn't even try. Instead he sniffed, whined, and retreated into the back seat.

"I told you he was well-trained," Melanie said. "He won't get out unless he's called."

"Care to bet? I expect it's the doggie bag he's feeling loyal to, not the rules."

"I don't bet," Melanie said.

The crowd began drifting away, except for a few diehards. Melanie answered questions and passed out business cards, but he thought she was starting to droop.

Finally Wyatt intervened. "Time to go. I'll drive."

"I thought you didn't drive antiques." But she was yawning, so the words weren't quite distinct.

By the time they got back to the yard, Melanie's eyes were closed and Scruffy had curled up in the back seat with his paws on the doggie bag.

Wyatt hated to wake her, but there was no alternative. "Melanie, do you want me to drop you somewhere?"

She said something indistinct.

"You're too nearly asleep to drive. I'll take you home if you can tell me how to get there."

She didn't answer.

He could hardly take her home when he didn't know where she lived. Maybe, he thought, the blast of chilly air when he got out of the car would wake her up enough to knock some sense into her. He pulled off the highway into the lot, parked the Ford, and opened the door. Cold wind swirled in.

Melanie's eyes snapped open and she sat up, shaking her head as if to clear it. "Thank you for dinner and everything. It wasn't a bad evening after all."

"I'm glad you enjoyed it," he said wryly. "I'll take you on home if you like. Just tell me where."

"No—I'll need a car in the morning anyway." She slid across the seat till she was behind the wheel and put the car into gear.

"I'll see you later, then," Wyatt said.

As the Ford pulled away, he crossed the lot to where

he'd left his car and flicked the remote to unlock the doors.

It wasn't a bad evening after all.

Well, he supposed there were worse verdicts. As far as that was concerned, if he were pressed, Wyatt would have to say much the same thing himself—the evening had turned out to be more pleasant than he'd expected. Melanie Stafford might be in the running to be named most disastrously honest woman of the year, but at least there wasn't a dull moment when she was around. On the other hand, she'd remained perfectly calm when Jennifer had made her grandstand gesture—which was more than he would have expected of most of the women he knew.

And on the dance floor, she'd been limber, yielding, graceful, seeming to anticipate his every move. *She dances like a lover...*

He caught himself just a little too late to bar from his mind the image of Melanie's lithe body wrapped around him—but not on a dance floor.

What was the matter with him? He'd known her less than twenty-four hours, and for two-thirds of that time he'd been ready to hire a hot-air balloon for the sheer pleasure of ascending to ten thousand feet and dumping her over the side. But for the other third of the day...

Go home, Reynolds. Maybe you'll wake up in the morning and discover it was all a nightmare.

He tried to start his car's engine, but nothing happened except a rapid clicking—the characteristic sound of a dead battery giving its feeble last effort. The trickle which it had put forth to unlock the doors seemed to be the last bit of strength it had possessed.

All that concern about whether she could get herself

home, he thought, *but she's safely tucked in and here you sit—stranded.*

He had raised the hood and was tinkering with the battery cables when the Ford drew up beside him and the driver's side window lowered. "That's always the problem with new cars," Melanie said sympathetically. "You're never prepared for it when something goes wrong."

Melanie didn't know what made her turn around two blocks from the yard and go back. She told herself it was a foolish impulse, that Wyatt would be long gone. Yet something was telling her to check, and she knew if she didn't follow her instincts, she wouldn't be able to sleep no matter how tired she was.

And sure enough, the car was still sitting there, with Wyatt leaning over the engine. She paused for a moment to admire the view of him from behind before letting the Ford creep up beside him so she could make a smart remark.

Wyatt didn't seem amused. "It's just the battery."

"Did you check the cables?"

"That's the first thing I looked at. There's no need for you to stick around."

"Hey, don't get grouchy with me. Just because you don't know what you're doing—"

"I'm not grouchy, and I do know what I'm doing."

"Guys are always grouchy when a woman comes along to rescue them."

"You don't have to rescue me. I'll call the motor club for a jump start."

"That's exactly what I mean. It's the middle of the night. You'll get the answering service, and it could be an hour before they wake somebody up and get them out here. And then, unless you drive around enough to recharge the battery, it'll likely be dead again in the morning. Let's run a drop cord out and put the charger on it, and you can take your choice of cars to get home.''

''I don't want to leave my car sitting out here with the hood open. If somebody doesn't steal the engine, they'll at least take the drop cord and the battery charger.''

''Well, I'm not helping you push it around the back of the building. So just let it sit till morning, and go grab another car.''

''I have a funny feeling about driving an antique vehicle across Kansas City at this hour of the night with nothing to prove that I actually own half of it.''

''Why?'' Melanie asked shrewdly. ''Was it stealing a car that got you the stretch at military school? Never mind. I'll write you a note if it'll make you feel better.''

''All right, you want the truth? I don't feel like struggling with another unfamiliar car at this hour.''

''Fine. You drove the Ford here, you can drive it home.''

''Then you'd have to wake up the mop and get into a cold car yourself.''

''It wouldn't be the first time.''

''I could drop you off,'' Wyatt offered.

''I told you already—I need a car in the morning and I hate waiting around for a ride. Get in, and I'll take you home.''

He didn't move. ''I live south of downtown, Melanie.'' There was a note of warning in his voice.

South of downtown Kansas City. That meant half an hour's drive each way, at least. *Me and my big mouth.* Melanie sighed. A deal was a deal. ''I said I'd take you, so I'll take you.''

"I'll call a cab."

"That will take just about as long as the motor club—if they find the place at all. You can't just sit here in the cold in the meantime."

"I'll go inside."

"Look, keep arguing and it'll be dawn before you get anything done."

In the back seat, Scruffy lifted his nose off the doggie bag and whined softly.

"The mop wants to go home, Melanie."

"So do I. All right, you can crash at my place till morning."

Wyatt's eyebrows lifted. "Are you sure I won't be a nuisance?"

She smiled. "You want the truth? You'll be a lot less of a nuisance there than if I have to drive you home. In the morning, the guys can tow the Baritsa in and work it over."

He didn't even flinch at the idea of turning Robbie and his crew loose on a new Baritsa. He must be starting to adjust, Melanie thought, and felt a tinge of regret—it wasn't going to be nearly as much fun to tease him now.

Wyatt walked around the Ford and got in. "Your guys work on Saturdays?"

"Half a day, at least. That's when the hobbyists come in for their parts."

Her bungalow was only a couple of miles away. As she pulled into the driveway, Scruffy sat up in the back seat and sighed as if in relief.

In the fading moonlight, the bungalow looked a little forlorn. There hadn't been time yet, or a pleasant enough day, for her to clean up winter's leftovers. Leaves had blown up against the foundation and tangled in the shrubs near the front door, and stubble from last autumn's chrysanthemums lined the flower beds by the driveway. Though Melanie noticed the debris every time she came home, tonight it seemed more untidy than usual. But perhaps that was only because of the long shadows.

"I didn't expect you to have a house," Wyatt said.

"I debated whether to sell it, after Mother died. It's a lot of upkeep—the flowers, especially. And now that there's just me, it's a bit big. But it's hard to find an apartment that will take the pets."

"You've got more than just the mop?"

"My mother had a couple of cats." She unlocked the front door, and two Siamese looked up from the seat of a deeply-cushioned chair. One yawned, the other closed his big blue eyes and snuggled deeper into the upholstery.

"There's an extra bedroom," she said. "Just let me run up and put sheets on—"

"Don't be ridiculous. Go to bed, Melanie. I'll just crash on the couch."

"You'll probably have cats all over you, and a dog crunching a bone at your feet."

"At least I won't feel lonely."

She started up the stairs. It felt odd, not being alone in her house. In the year since her mother died, she hadn't had an overnight guest.

Of course, she thought, it would have felt even more odd if he'd been coming upstairs with her...odd, and awkward.

It was sensitive of him to realize that and sidestep the problem. Unless it wasn't her feelings he was watching out for, but his own safety.

Sure, she mocked herself. *He probably thinks you're trying to lure him upstairs to your bedroom!*

* * *

The morning was so gray and gloomy that the cats didn't bother to wake up when Wyatt let the mop out into the fenced backyard. He found the makings for a pot of coffee, waited for it to brew, let the mop back in, drank a cup, but still there was no hint of movement from the second floor. It was almost nine, and Melanie had apparently not stirred.

Finally he got a second mug from the cabinet, filled it, and climbed the stairs.

It was utterly stupid, he told himself, to feel like a burglar. Just because he was exploring an unfamiliar house, one he hadn't been invited to roam through, it didn't mean he was doing anything wrong. She might be sick up there. Helpless.

There were half a dozen doors opening off the small hallway at the top of the stairs, and all of them were closed. Wyatt knocked on the first one, waited, and opened it a crack to discover a linen closet. Then he realized that the mop had followed him upstairs and was waiting expectantly at the far side of the hall, beside a door that looked just like all the others.

Wyatt was just reaching out to tap a knuckle against the wood when the dog reared up and nudged the doorknob with his nose. The door swung open as Wyatt touched it. The dog romped in, and Wyatt heard a muffled, wordless groan from the bed.

All he could see was a long, formless figure buried under the blankets. The curtains were closed and the room was dim except for a night-light in the shape of a seashell, low on the wall beside the bed. "Melanie?"

The cats had been asleep downstairs when he'd poured the coffee, but they must have joined the procession while he'd been knocking on the linen closet—

trying in vain to wake the sheets and towels. One of the Siamese hissed and darted under his raised foot; the other zoomed across the room, ruffling up a rug.

Wyatt tried to keep from stepping on the cat's tail, caught his toe on the rug, and started a forward flip that was abruptly interrupted when his elbows hit the edge of the bed. The coffee mug stayed firmly gripped in his hand, but the contents soared in an airborne puddle, hovered, and descended.

Melanie shot up from the blankets.

His eyes were quickly adjusting to the dim light, so he could see coffee dripping from her hair, beading on her eyelashes, and forming an irregular pattern like spattered brown paint across the front of her white pajamas. She took a deep breath.

Now you're in for it, Reynolds. The coffee might not have been hot enough to burn, but I bet her tongue will leave blisters.

"Thanks," she said. Her voice was still sleep-roughened. It was very low, very raspy, very sexy. "You've given me exactly what I wanted this morning, Wyatt—coffee and a hot shower. How efficient of you to combine them."

CHAPTER FIVE

HE STARTED to apologize—or perhaps, Melanie thought, he was trying to explain. She used the corner of the sheet to wipe her eyes. "This should be quite some story, and I'll be happy to listen to it—as soon as I'm not dripping coffee. I'd especially like to know how you ended up without a drop on you while I must look like I'm entered in a wet T-shirt contest."

His gaze dropped to her coffee-spattered pajama jacket, and he shook his head. "Not wet. Just damp." He sounded almost disappointed.

"Then next time you'll have to remember to use a larger mug." Her voice grew a little sharper. "If you don't mind getting out of my bed, Wyatt—"

"Oh. Sure. I'll be downstairs."

The pressure of his elbows as he pushed himself up off the bed rocked the mattress a little. It was utterly silly, Melanie told herself, to feel just a tiny bit seasick at the sensation.

As soon as he was gone, she climbed out of the soggy bed. She stripped off the sheets, intending to start the washing machine before she left for work. But when she came back from her shower and for the first time noticed the clock on her bedside table, the bundle of sheets was forgotten.

How could she have slept so long? She never over-slept—not even when she'd been up late, not even when the morning was gloomy enough that it looked as if dawn hadn't yet broken.

74

She thundered down the stairs and into the kitchen. "What's the matter with you? Why didn't you tell me what time it is?"

"That's what I was attempting to do when the cats got in the way," Wyatt said. "What did you think I was up to? Trying to seduce you with breakfast in bed?"

That's one in the eye for you, Stafford, Melanie thought. *Seduction would be the last thing on his mind.*

"I figured, considering the rate you drink coffee at work, you'd be less likely to kill the messenger if I was carrying caffeine. But things went a little wrong." He handed her a mug. "Be careful with this one, it's fresh—and hotter."

The liquid in the mug was steaming. "Do I need to remind you that I'm not the one who spilled the last cup?"

"Maybe we should just start over." Wyatt's voice was mild. "Good morning, Melanie. I hope you slept well."

"Just fine," she muttered. "Come on, let's go."

"I thought you said the shop's only open a half day on Saturday."

"Yes, but we aim for it to be the *first* half of the day." She swallowed her coffee and set the mug aside.

They weren't simply late. They were so late, compared to Melanie's normal starting time, that the shop crew should have been at work long since. But she had forgotten about the Baritsa, parked smack in the middle of the lot where Robbie and the guys couldn't have helped noticing it and wondering why it was there.

The Baritsa was the first thing that caught her eye when she turned off the highway, but the second thing she saw was a row of faces pressed to the glass overlooking the parking lot.

By the time she parked the car, the faces had disappeared from the window, and when they walked into the showroom Robbie was pouring himself a cup of coffee, one of his guys was straightening up the pictures on the bulletin board—an occupation she'd never known to attract his interest before—and the third man was fiddling with the hood ornament of the little green roadster. None of them looked at Melanie and Wyatt.

"How considerate of you, Melanie," Wyatt murmured in her ear. "Since you didn't want the employees to be worried about their jobs, you gave them something else to think about."

"I don't need any trouble from you," she growled.

"Man, that's some bark you've got." He pulled back in obviously-feigned apprehension. "Did the mop teach you how to do that, or did you teach him?"

Scruffy had apparently figured out that he'd acquired a new name, for he perked up, sat up on his haunches, laid a paw on Wyatt's ankle, and stared up adoringly at him.

"Hey," Wyatt told the dog. "Since when did I say I wanted you worshiping at my feet?"

"That's what you get for giving him steak bones in the middle of the night," Melanie gibed.

Wyatt grinned. She saw the silver shimmer of his eyes and winced, knowing that she'd put her foot in her mouth—but good.

"You're right, sweetheart," he said softly. "You *don't* need any trouble from me. You can create plenty all by yourself."

She sneaked a look around at her employees. All three of them were staring at her, their jaws lax as they took in the implications of Wyatt being anywhere near her dog in the middle of the night.

Of course they drew the obvious conclusion, she thought irritably. *They're guys. What did you expect?*

She tried to keep her voice casual. "Wyatt's car wouldn't start last night, so he camped out on my couch. Now he's anxious to get home."

"I wouldn't be so sure about that," the guy at the bulletin board said under his breath.

Melanie ignored him. "I know you're short-handed because it's Saturday, Robbie, but can you spring one of the guys to charge the battery and check the car over? There was no obvious reason for it to be dead."

The guy standing beside the roadster grinned and gave Wyatt a thumbs-up signal.

Melanie pretended not to have seen it and stalked past him into her office. The mail was already on her desk. She turned the computer on and began to flip through the envelopes.

Wyatt followed her.

"Leave the door open," she ordered. "The last thing I need is a crew out there wondering what's going on in here."

"Nothing they'd want to watch. We need to do a dry-run of the charity package before we give your friend Erika the details."

"Sorority sister," Melanie corrected. "She was never my friend."

"Whatever. Anyway, we can check out the arrangements with the restaurant and show off a car again all at the same time. Is tonight all right with you?"

"No. I'm not doing a repeat of last night."

"Of course not. Felicity's is an entirely different—"

"I mean I already have plans for the evening."

"We could do lunch instead."

"I'll be here through the lunch hour, working." She

slit open an envelope and extracted a check. "Besides, don't you have anything better to do? Like patching things up with Jennifer?"

"I wondered how long it would take you to ask about that."

"Who's asking? I'm only commenting that it appeared some fence-mending might be in order—unless she comes from some country I've never heard of, where a slap across the face is a form of greeting."

Wyatt snapped his fingers. "That must be it. I've always thought Jennifer didn't seem to inhabit the same planet as the rest of us."

Which of course told Melanie precisely nothing. *What did you expect—that he'd pour out his heart? Maybe even ask your advice?*

"Well, if she's an alien that makes her just about a perfect match for Jackson." She shot a look at him, but Wyatt looked only mildly interested, as if the whole subject had nothing to do with him.

Melanie turned her chair around to the computer to check if any parts orders had come in overnight. "I'm surprised you're not out watching your precious Baritsa, just to be sure the guys aren't injuring it."

"I have infinite trust in Robbie's crew. Be careful, Melanie—you're beginning to sound as if you don't want me around."

"Brilliant deduction, Sherlock."

"Last night," he murmured, "you wanted me to stay."

"Well, last night, you—" She looked up at a tap on the open door. "Never mind. What is it, Robbie?"

"I've looked at the Baritsa, sir. If you'd like to come out, I'll show you what I found."

"That sounds ominous," Wyatt said. But he slid off

the corner of the desk and followed Robbie across the showroom.

Melanie printed out a couple of orders and took them out to the shop. "Fred, when you get a chance, pull these parts and leave them on the workbench by the back door—I need them in time for Monday's shipment."

When she got back to the office, Wyatt was in her chair, using the phone. She considered sitting down across from him to finish the mail, and decided not to bother. "Bath time, Scruff," she said.

The dog leaped out of his basket and was waiting at the shop door when Melanie got there. He was almost vibrating with eagerness. "You know what day it is, don't you, pal?" She cleared out the deep utility sink which stood in a far corner of the shop and started to fill it with warm, sudsy water.

Before it was full, Wyatt had followed her. He studied Scruffy, who was sitting up on a tall stool, impatiently waiting for the sink to fill. "You're absolutely certain this is a dog? I've never seen one who didn't run the other direction at the mere mention of a bath."

"But then you don't know Scruff very well. The doggie bag may have seemed an easy route to his heart, but really he's far deeper than that." She turned the water off.

Scruffy stepped carefully into the sink.

"Good boy," Melanie told him. "Not even a splash—unlike some people I know, who can give an entirely new meaning to the simple phrase, 'Join me in a cup of coffee.' What's the verdict on the car?"

"Robbie says it's a faulty alternator. They're recharging the battery now."

"What good is that going to do?" She reached for a bottle of pet shampoo from the shelf above the sink. "If the alternator isn't working, it'll just drain the power again as soon as you start the engine.''

"Robbie thinks if I'm careful I can drive it to the dealership.'' He perched on the stool that Scruffy had just vacated.

"What if it croaks in the middle of a traffic lane? Have we considered the advantages of calling a tow truck instead?''

Wyatt didn't miss a beat. "What a good idea, Melanie. If I have it hauled in, I can stay here and help you for the rest of the day.''

"On second thought, it would leave a terrible impression—a broken-down, brand-new Baritsa being dragged down the highway by a wrecker. Definitely you should drive it.''

"I thought that's what you'd say. You'll be happy to know Fred has volunteered to follow me in case Robbie's wrong and it dies on the way.''

"That's a shame. I mean, what a good idea. We wouldn't want you to be stranded.''

Wyatt grinned. "Since we're not going to Felicity's tonight—''

"You may do whatever you like,'' Melanie pointed out. "I merely said I was already busy.''

"It occurs to me that I'm the one who's come up with all the promotional plans so far. If you don't like my ideas, what do you want to do instead?''

"How about going to a drive-in movie?''

"I didn't know there were any still operating. Besides, it's a little early—and chilly—for them to be running.''

Melanie shrugged. "That's the extent of my ideas.'' She squeezed suds out of Scruffy's coat and pulled the drain plug. Then she adjusted the spray nozzle and began rinsing him from head to tail. Scruffy stretched his neck out blissfully.

"Does the mop have a date tonight?"

Melanie nodded. "He's going visiting." She turned the water off and reached for a towel. "All right, Scruff. No rolling in the dirt until I give you permission."

The dog gave a short yelp. Wyatt moved off the stool and Scruffy leaped down and gave himself a good head-to-tail shake.

Wyatt looked concerned. "You're not going to dry him off any more than that? I'd hate to see the mop come down with a head cold."

"You catch cold from a virus, Wyatt, not from the outside temperature. Besides, if I'd blow-dry his coat, he'd end up resembling a powder puff."

"I can't see it would be any worse than looking like a mop. At least he'd be warm."

The back door opened and Fred came in with a head-light and a cable which he set carefully on the work-bench. "There are the pieces you needed, Melanie. Are you ready to go, Mr. Reynolds? Robbie says your battery's got about as much of a charge as he can give it."

"Have a good time," Melanie murmured. "Oh, and Wyatt? Don't call me for a ride."

Wyatt did call, however, to let her know that he'd arrived safely at the repair shop. Very soberly and with almost no irony in her voice, Melanie thanked him for his thoughtfulness, and he laughed and said he'd see her on Monday. "I was afraid of that," she muttered, but he'd already hung up.

She put the phone down and shook her head in puzzlement. Was it actually only two days since he'd first turned up? It seemed barely possible. The man was like a migraine—annoying, unpredictable, and—once started—impossible to ignore.

A tall brunette who'd come in while Melanie was on the phone said, "What's the deal, Melanie? It's not like you to go around muttering to yourself."

It is now that Wyatt's hanging around, Melanie thought. "Hi, Angie. Robbie's out in the lot somewhere."

"I saw him. We're going to the zoo as soon as he's finished, so I decided to come on in and change Luke's diaper while I waited. Mind if I use the hood of the car?" She set the baby carrier down beside the roadster.

"I'm sure it's seen worse in its day."

Angie laid a changing pad on the car, unstrapped the baby from the carrier, and lifted him out. He gurgled and waved his arms and tried to escape by rolling over, and she pinned him with one hand while she unfastened his romper with the other. "Can you hand me a diaper?" she asked. "I forgot to allow for the slope of the hood."

Melanie dug in Angie's bag and then took hold of Luke's little hands while Angie worked. "Hey, there, big boy. Why haven't you come in lately to flirt with me?"

Luke grinned and babbled.

"He's grown so much, Angie."

"Nineteen pounds," Angie said. "And he's starting to walk around things—hanging on, of course. One of these days he's going to take off and run, and there will be no keeping up with him." She fastened the last snap and Melanie picked the baby up and snuggled him close.

But Luke wasn't in the mood to snuggle. He leaned out of her arms, trying to reach the hood ornament on the roadster.

"Boys and their toys," Angie said ruefully. "I had

no idea the obsession with cars started before their first birthday. No, Luke, Melanie doesn't want your finger-prints all over that shiny new wax job.''

"Go for it, Luke. Show me how well you can walk.'' Melanie set the baby down. He grinned, planted both chubby hands against the polished surface of the car door and began to work his way around on unsteady feet.

Angie leaned against the fender. "So was that the new guy in your life?''

Melanie was momentarily at a loss.

"The one who was on the phone when I came in,'' Angie explained. "Robbie told me—''

"About Wyatt owning half the place now? That makes him the new guy in all our lives.''

"No, Robbie didn't mention that part.''

"He didn't? Then what was he talking about?''

"The fact that the two of you came in together this morning.''

Melanie groaned. "I thought guys never talked about that kind of stuff.''

"Well, it does have to be pretty juicy before they get interested. Of course, I don't believe everything Robbie told me. Just because what's-his-name—Wyatt, did you say?—left his car here overnight and you came in very late and you made it such a point to talk about him sleeping on the couch that only an idiot would have bought the story—''

"Is that what Robbie told you? I'll...'' Melanie couldn't think of any payback that was quite horrible enough. "I'll make him polish every last inch of rust off that Dodge that's sitting behind the building.''

Angie laughed. "The one that doesn't even have an engine? Ooh, that'll scare him into silence all right. So what really happened? Dish it out, Melanie—it's just us girls now. If you tell me this guy didn't get within twenty feet of your bed, I'll take your word for it.''

Melanie opened her mouth and closed it again. She could say that Wyatt hadn't been anywhere close to her bed, but that would be lying. However, if she told the literal truth, nobody would believe it.

And if she even started to explain why they'd gone to the club together last night, she'd have to admit the business was for sale. So much for not wanting to cause her employees premature concern about their jobs.

No, the whole thing was just too complicated to explain—and what had happened in her bedroom this morning was nobody's business anyway. ''I didn't sleep with him, if that's what you're asking.''

Angie grinned. ''Well, Robbie did say you looked as if you hadn't had a wink of sleep.''

''You have a dirty mind, Angie. There's nothing going on. Honest.''

The door opened, and Melanie, relieved at the interruption, turned to greet the newcomer. With any luck it would be a last-minute customer and by the time she was finished Robbie would have swept his wife and son off to the zoo.

But instead the man who came in was wearing the uniform of Kansas City's best-known department store, and he was carrying an enormous bundle that barely fit through the door.

''I didn't know Tyler-Royale had started shipping car parts,'' Angie murmured. There was an undercurrent of amusement in her voice. ''So this must be a morning-after gift.''

''Probably some kind of token thank-you for putting him up last night. And putting up with him.''

''Pretty big to be a mere token.''

The deliveryman looked from one woman to the other. "Which of you is Ms. Stafford?"

Melanie took a half step forward.

"Will you sign for this package, please?"

Angie was right; it didn't look like a token. The package was too square to be flowers. And it was too huge to be a box of chocolates—unless for some unfathomable reason he'd had the store pack it in a cloud of foam.

Melanie's instincts told her it was too large to be anything but trouble.

She signed her name in an uncharacteristic scrawl and the deliveryman handed her the bundle and went away.

The package was heavier than she'd expected, considering how bulky it was. It was soft, too—there was no box under the silvery-blue wrapping paper, just some squishy, formless object. An enormous teddy bear, perhaps, curled up in a fetal position?

She gritted her teeth and tore off the wrappings.

"Is that a sleeping bag?" Angie asked in disbelief.

Whatever it was, it was white, quilted and puffy. Melanie shook it out, and several smaller packages which had been folded inside fell out. "It's a down comforter."

"Nice." Angie stooped to pick up one of the fallen packages. "Egyptian cotton pillowcases, and sheets to match."

Of course, Melanie thought. He'd practically destroyed her bed this morning, so he was making up for it. It was rather sweet of him, actually, to realize that the coffee stains might never come out of her sheets. Wyatt might be problematic to deal with sometimes, but he was certainly a gentleman...

"Oh, look." Angie swooped. "There's a card, too."

Foreboding flooded over Melanie. "Give me that!" she demanded.

But it was too late. The card was not in an envelope, and it had fallen face-up. Only a saint could have picked it up off the showroom floor without reading it, and no one who knew Angie would ever mistake her for Francis of Assisi. Her eyes went wide, and she handed the card over without a word.

To make up for spilling coffee in your bed, Wyatt had written.

Melanie wanted to shriek. She'd actually given him the benefit of the doubt for a minute, calling him a gentleman. What a fool she'd been! *I'll tear the sheets into strips, braid them into a rope, and use it to hang him.*

"There's nothing going on," Angie murmured. "Right."

Dusk was falling as Melanie parked the ten-year-old Chevy at the far corner of the hospital lot and opened the bag which contained Scruffy's equipment. In his excitement, the dog bounced over the seat and practically into her lap. "Enough," she ordered. "You have to calm down before you can go in."

He stood still, but he was still quivering with exhilaration as she fitted the green harness-vest over his shoulders and buckled it around his front legs. Once it was on, however, he calmed.

She fastened his leash to the ring on the back of the vest and walked across the lot and in the main door.

In the lobby, a stout woman spotted them and did a double take. "Well, I never!" she said loudly. "The very idea of bringing a dog into a hospital!" She put out her foot as if to push Scruffy aside.

Melanie shortened the leash and held her breath. If

Scruffy so much as growled inside the hospital—not that she'd blame him, because the woman had almost kicked him—he'd be out in a flash and he'd never be allowed to come back.

Instead, he held his head high and trotted in a dignified silence straight toward the elevator.

"Some people have no idea what's appropriate," the woman sniffed.

"Quite right," Melanie said over her shoulder, and pushed the elevator button. "And you're one of them," she finished under her breath.

On the sixth floor, she turned down the neon-striped hallway and stopped at the nurses' station to sign in. "Hello, Melanie," said a nurse in a red-plaid lab coat. "The dinner trays just went back down to the kitchen, and the kids are waiting for you in the schoolroom."

"They're not waiting for me, Janice. It's my pal here that they're anxious to see." Melanie lengthened Scruffy's leash a little, and he tugged eagerly.

She paused at the door of the schoolroom, as she always had to in order to adjust her thoughts. No matter what the hospital called it, the room was scarcely the kind to be found in any ordinary elementary school. It was brightly painted, with the alphabet displayed on one wall and a bulletin board full of drawings on another. There were small tables and bookshelves and drawing easels. But there were also wheelchairs and oxygen hookups, and the toys were mostly the sort that could be run through a sterilizer in order to protect the patients from infection.

Each week when she and Scruffy came there was a different mix of kids, as they came and went for their treatments. Today there were some familiar faces—Madison was back again, working a puzzle on the floor with an IV pole standing beside her. Jimmy was still there, though he looked better than he had last week; today he was sitting up by himself, not propped with pillows. And Andrea was there as well; her hair was starting to grow back, Melanie noted. There were also three children she hadn't seen before.

Scruffy stood quietly at the door, looking around the room. Then he pulled gently until Melanie followed him over to a small, wan-faced boy in a wheelchair, one of the newcomers. The dog sat on the rug in front of the chair and politely offered a paw.

"This is Scruffy," Melanie said. "He's come to visit."

The boy reached out a tentative finger to touch the dog. "Why is he wearing that jacket?"

"It's like a uniform," Melanie explained. "It helps him remember to use his best manners, and it helps everyone else remember to touch him gently."

"Does he like coming to the hospital?" The child looked sideways up at her. "I don't."

Melanie's heart twisted. "He likes to help sick people feel better, and sometimes just petting him does that."

"How?" The boy's tone was scornful.

"Want to try it?" Melanie looked around for an aide. "Will you hand me Scruffy's bench, please?"

"Is that his name?" the boy asked. "Scruffy? It doesn't sound very nice."

"Well, he wasn't very nice-looking when he first came to live with me, so it seemed to fit him." Melanie set the small carpeted platform next to the wheelchair. Scruffy jumped up on it, turned round, and lay down, his nose tucked between his paws. The bench put his back at exactly the right height for a child who was sitting in a chair, in order to pet him with the least possible exertion. The boy's hand fell almost automatically onto Scruffy's coat, and his fingers trembled as he began to stroke the soft fur.

Melanie backed off, still holding the leash and closely watching the child and the dog, but giving them as much privacy as possible.

"Amazing," the aide said under her breath. "That dog always goes straight to the sickest one in the room. It's like he can smell them." She moved off to help Madison reposition her IV pole.

Slowly, Scruffy moved around the room, setting his own pace as he visited each child for a few minutes and then moved on to the next.

Midway through the evening, as Scruffy was playing a very gentle tug-of-war with Jimmy, the nurse came into the playroom. "Ten minute warning, everybody," she said. "As soon as Dr. Scruffy finishes his rounds, it'll be time for snacks and bed."

For the first time, the schoolroom sounded almost normal, as the kids groaned and complained. Only the little boy in the wheelchair didn't seem to hear; he was sitting up a little straighter and still watching Scruffy, and suddenly the dog stopped pulling on the rope toy, nuzzled Jimmy gently, and came back to climb up on the bench beside the wheelchair. The child sighed, laid a hand on Scruffy's coat, and closed his eyes.

The nurse came across the room. "We ordered ice cream for you too, Scruff."

The dog's eyes brightened and his tail wagged, but he didn't move away from the child.

"You spoil him, Janice."

The nurse laughed. "Look who's talking. Thanks for coming, Melanie. It's always easier to get them to sleep after Scruffy's been here. I'd have expected it to be the other way around, but he doesn't rev them up, he relaxes them. Same time next week?''

Melanie didn't answer. ''Janice, is Andrea all right?''

''She's doing fine. She's just here for a last round of chemo. Why?''

Melanie shrugged. ''I don't know. Just a silly feeling, I guess.''

Janice pulled an electronic thermometer out of the pocket of her lab coat and crossed the room. Less than ten seconds later, she put the thermometer back, ruffled the stubble of hair on Andrea's head, and came back to Melanie. ''How did you know she was running a degree high? You're incredible.''

Melanie shrugged. ''You'd have caught it when you put her to bed.''

''Yes, but you've given us an extra half hour's start on whatever infection she's picked up. Scruffy's not the only one who has an instinct for dealing with sick kids. In fact, I'm pretty well convinced he learned it from you.'' Janice's eyes were full of compassion. ''You have a gift, Melanie, and you know it's a crime not to use it.''

The words echoed through Melanie's head as she drove home, and as she brushed Scruffy's coat where the uniform-vest had matted it, and as she made up her bed with brand-new Egyptian cotton.

She'd told herself for three years that she'd come to terms with giving up her dream. But in fact, it hadn't taken much to bring it back to life. Wyatt's suggestion that they sell the business, salted with Erika's snippy assumption that Melanie was dealing in cars because she couldn't do anything else, and topped off tonight with Janice's insight…

You have a gift, and you know it's a crime not to use it.

The question was, what was she going to do about it?

CHAPTER SIX

SUNDAY dawned bright and beautiful, the most spring-like day so far. When Wyatt pulled up in Melanie's driveway, he wasn't surprised to see her on her knees in a flower bed with a heap of winter debris beside her.

As he got out of the car, she sat back on her heels and watched him. At least, she seemed to be watching him, but it was hard to tell where she was looking because of the oversize sunglasses she was wearing. Between the glasses, the wide-brimmed hat which shielded her face, and the gauntlet-like gloves she wore, she looked smaller and much more fragile than the dynamo who had taken him on head to head when he'd first walked into the shop.

"It's not Monday," she said, and turned back to the flower bed. "You said you'd see me on Monday."

"I said I'd see you at the shop on Monday," he corrected.

"Don't you have anything better to do than hang around annoying me?"

Her words were tart, but the tone wasn't. Wyatt thought she sounded tired. "As a matter of fact," he said, "yes."

"Oh."

"You thought I didn't work?"

"I was starting to wonder if the flour mills ran entirely by remote control."

"I never had anything to do with the flour mills. I told you I was a twig on that family tree, if you remember."

"You'll pardon me for getting mixed up. So what brought you here today?"

"I couldn't stay away." He let a teasing note creep into his voice, but he was very nearly telling the truth. He'd awakened this morning thinking of yesterday's unfinished conversation about what they could do to promote the business. If her best effort was the suggestion that they go to a drive-in movie, for heaven's sake—

Melanie gave a little snort of disbelief.

"Actually, I tried to call, but you didn't answer your phone." He squatted down beside the flower bed and watched the rhythmic, almost mechanical movement of her hands. He could see green spikes poking through the freshly turned dirt. "What are you planting?"

"Nothing. I'm just clearing off last year's dead growth so the perennials don't have to compete with it as they come out of hibernation. Haven't you ever seen a crocus before?"

"I think I saw some once in a pot at the florist's shop."

"Where you were no doubt buying roses."

"What's wrong with roses?"

"Nothing, if you're looking for short-term perfection followed by immediate decay. Personally, I prefer flowers that last. I see you got your car fixed."

"Runs like a charm. Did you call Brad Edwards yesterday about the Ford?"

"I tried, but I only got his voice mail. I left a message."

"How much did you tell him you wanted for the car?"

"I didn't—I just asked him to call me. Whether he will or not is another question. I wish you would have let me cut a deal right then, when he was in the mood."

"He'll call."

"I hope you're right." She sneezed and made a face. "It's supposed to be too early for pollen. At this rate, it's going to be a horrible year for people with allergies." She shifted her position a couple of feet and began weeding again.

"Maybe the mop gave you a cold."

"People don't catch diseases from dogs any more than they do from getting chilled. Not if the dogs are clean."

"That explains you giving the mop a bath yesterday."

Her hands stilled for a moment.

He wondered why it was such a big deal. "Fred told me what you do on Saturday nights."

"Fred talks a lot."

"Why try to keep it a secret?"

"I don't. But some people think it's silly, and others think it's downright disgusting. The ones who approve think I'm some kind of a saint, and that's just as crazy."

Because it makes you even more uncomfortable than the ones who disapprove, Wyatt thought. *That explains it.* "So you don't say much about it."

"Not any more."

He pushed a pile of debris out of her way. "How did you get the idea of taking the dog to visit kids in the hospital in the first place? And how did you train him?"

"I didn't train him. Whenever I took him for a walk in the park, he'd seek out the sick kids. It took me a while to figure out what he was doing. Even after I was sure, it wasn't easy to convince the hospital, though I'd been volunteering there myself for quite a while. But once he proved himself—"

Wyatt looked over at the dog, who was sunning himself on the lawn and watching a squirrel in a nearby tree as if debating whether the excitement of the chase would be worth the effort of getting up. *Okay, he's a smart mop, but he's still a mop.*

"Where'd you get this extraordinary animal?"

Melanie shrugged. "He just wandered into the parking lot one Saturday to drink out of a puddle. No collar, no tags—he was a skeleton with hair. If you think he looks like a mop now, you should have seen him then, because he looked like he'd been used to scrub out a grease pit."

"So you took him home."

"I fully intended to clean him up and drop him off at the animal shelter when it opened again on Monday. Of course, that was two years ago and I haven't gotten around to calling them yet."

Wyatt grinned. "It sounds as if sick people aren't the only kind he can sniff out. You know, Melanie, this is a great story. Maybe we could get some publicity. Scruffy the junkyard dog developing this incredible talent—"

"You are not going to turn those kids into a publicity stunt." Her voice was firm.

"Sorry. I guess I didn't think about that part. I'm just trying my best to get some attention here, and so far you're not helping much. How about throwing a reunion?"

"What do you mean?"

"All the photos on that bulletin board in the showroom are of cars you've restored, right? I don't even have to ask if you still have the owners' addresses. I think we should invite them all to a reunion. Get all the cars back together."

"I'm sure they'll have a great time catching up on old times," Melanie said dryly. "Comparing odometers, gossiping about their owners, bragging about all the places they've been—"

"Drawing far more attention as a group than any one of them would individually."

"It sounds like it might be fun, but we don't have room. Did you count those pictures? There are more than fifty cars."

"We could clean out that back corner of the lot, which needs doing anyway. Or we could rent a big building somewhere, park all the cars inside, and charge admission to walk through and look at them."

"The owners would want a cut. If the cars are the big attraction—"

"They wouldn't expect anything if the ticket price goes to charity—like to your sick kids. Does that still count as turning them into a publicity stunt?"

"Probably. I don't know, Wyatt. I've been thinking about it, and I believe you're looking in the wrong place."

Wyatt shifted into a sitting position, reached for a paper bag she'd set off to the side, and began stuffing dead leaves into it. "I'm listening."

"You know people who have the money to buy it—but let's face it, not many of them are interested. Showing off at the clubs and restaurants may sell a car now and then, but it's not likely to get the attention of someone who wants the whole business."

"Unless Brad's starting up a whole string of theme nightclubs—"

"In the best-case scenario—which is a pretty wild dream—we might sell him half a dozen cars. It still wouldn't be like selling the whole operation."

"You're saying we need to hook up with a major collector."

Melanie shook her head. "No. You don't know car collectors, but I do. They're choosy. These people will hold out for years in order to get just the car they want rather than buying one that's almost like it. And the ones who can afford more than one classic car are still pretty particular about what they buy. They may want only Corvettes, or only cars from before the Depression, or only convertibles—but whatever their specialty is, they stick to it.''

''They take it so very seriously?''

''You'd better believe it. Some of them collect more than one kind of car, of course, and a few don't have any obvious theme. They buy whatever strikes their fancy—but even then, they're selective. Not everything appeals to them.''

''You're saying they don't buy old cars just because they're old.''

''Exactly. None of them want to end up with an odd assortment.''

''Which is what we've got.''

She nodded. ''That's why I think a collector isn't going to be seriously interested, because there's only so much bartering and trading they'll bother with. We need someone who knows cars, but who is more interested in buying and selling than in keeping them all. Someone who wants to keep the business running.''

''Unless we advertise it, I don't see how you're going to find this magical person who has money and business sense *and* likes old cars.''

Her shoulders drooped. ''I suppose you're right.''

Wyatt let the silence draw out. ''I know you're worried about the guys, Melanie, but they're going to find out sooner or later. It would be better to tell them up front than to let them get a nasty shock via the grapevine.''

An Important Message from the Editors

Dear Reader,

Because you've chosen to read one of our fine romance novels, we'd like to say "thank you!" And, as a special way to thank you, we've selected two more of the books you love so well, plus an exciting Mystery Gift, to send you absolutely FREE!

Please enjoy them with our compliments...

Pam Powers

Peel off Seal and Place Inside

EDITOR'S
FREE GIFT
SEAL
THANK YOU

How to validate your Editor's
FREE GIFT
"Thank You"

1. Peel off gift seal from front cover. Place it in space provided at right. This automatically entitles you to receive 2 FREE BOOKS and a fabulous mystery gift.

2. Send back this card and you'll get 2 brand-new Harlequin Romance® novels. These books have a cover price of $3.99 each in the U.S. and $4.50 each in Canada, but they are yours to keep absolutely free.

3. There's no catch. You're under no obligation to buy anything. We charge nothing—ZERO—for your first shipment. And you don't have to make any minimum number of purchases—not even one!

4. The fact is, thousands of readers enjoy receiving their books by mail from the Harlequin Reader Service®. They enjoy the convenience of home delivery...they like getting the best new novels at discount prices BEFORE they're available in stores...and they love their *Heart to Heart* subscriber newsletter featuring author news, horoscopes, recipes, book reviews and much more!

5. We hope that after receiving your free books you'll want to remain a subscriber. But the choice is yours— to continue or cancel, any time at all! So why not take us up on our invitation, with no risk of any kind. You'll be glad you did!

6. Remember...just for validating your Editor's Free Gift Offer, we'll send you THREE gifts, *ABSOLUTELY FREE!*

GET A *Free* MYSTERY GIFT...

SURPRISE MYSTERY GIFT COULD BE YOURS _FREE_ AS A SPECIAL "THANK YOU" FROM THE EDITORS OF HARLEQUIN

Visit us online at
www.eHarlequin.com

The Editor's "Thank You" Free Gifts Include:

- Two BRAND-NEW romance novels!
- An exciting mystery gift!

PLACE FREE GIFT SEAL HERE

Yes I have placed my Editor's "Thank You" seal in the space provided above. Please send me 2 free books and a fabulous Mystery Gift. I understand I am under no obligation to purchase any books, as explained on the back and on the opposite page.

386 HDL DZ6S   186 HDL DZ67

FIRST NAME	LAST NAME

ADDRESS

APT.#	CITY

STATE/PROV.	ZIP/POSTAL CODE

(H-R-06/04)

Thank You!

The Harlequin Reader Service® — Here's how it works:

Accepting your 2 free books and gift places you under no obligation to buy anything. You may keep the books and gift and return the shipping statement marked "cancel." If you do not cancel, about a month later we'll send you 6 additional books and bill you just $3.34 each in the U.S., or $3.80 each in Canada, plus 25¢ shipping & handling per book and applicable taxes if any.* That's the complete price and — compared to cover prices of $3.99 each in the U.S. and $4.50 each in Canada — it's quite a bargain! You may cancel at any time, but if you choose to continue, every month we'll send you 6 more books, which you may either purchase at the discount price or return to us and cancel your subscription.

*Terms and prices subject to change without notice. Sales tax applicable in N.Y. Canadian residents will be charged applicable provincial taxes and GST.

She nodded again—but this time it was more auto-matic reaction than agreement, he thought.

"You know," he said, "instead of being scared out of their wits, they might appreciate the warning so they can get prepared."

"You may be right about that. But it wasn't the guys I was thinking about just now. The minute we advertise that the business is for sale, the restoration trade will drop like a rock. Nobody's going to bring in a car for months and months of work if they don't know who they'll be dealing with by the time it's done."

She had a point, he admitted. "If you've got an al-ternative to suggest—"

"And even worse, if we list it and then it doesn't sell, we'll have taken the hit for nothing. Wyatt, am I fooling myself to think anybody will even be interested?"

I sincerely hope not. "Someone will buy it, Melanie."

She looked up from the flower bed. "Of course you're right. I'd almost forgotten that you wanted it—at least for a while."

I wouldn't go quite that far.

"So someone else surely will too. Funny—it's only been a few days. How could it have slipped my mind that you bought it?" She took a deep breath. "I'm afraid I don't have any great plans to offer, but maybe this reunion idea of yours isn't so bad after all. People who are interested in cars all hang out together, and there's a good chance one of them will know someone who's interested in making a business of it."

"If you start asking around," he warned, "the word will get back to your guys pretty quickly."

She sighed. "Okay. I'll tell them tomorrow." She loosened the dirt around a pale green spike. "I'm really sorry that it didn't work out, Wyatt. I mean, that the business didn't turn out to be what you expected when you made the deal with Jackson.''

"It's my own fault for not looking further ahead.''

"Well—yes, it is. But I'm sure that's no comfort to you.''

She'd hit that nail squarely on the head, he thought. It wasn't any comfort at all.

By midday Monday, Melanie was not only sneezing regularly but her head was stuffy and her throat was sore. "So much for your diagnostic capabilities, Scruffy,'' she told the dog, who was sitting at her feet as she swallowed an aspirin from the first-aid kit. "Why didn't you tell me yesterday I was coming down with an old-fashioned head cold and not just spring allergies?''

Scruffy gave one short bark, as if protesting the slur on his reputation.

Melanie took a second aspirin and made a mental note to restock the bottle.

Robbie eyed her with concern. "Maybe you should go home,'' he suggested warily.

"I can't. I have too much to do, and I'm waiting for a call.'' Not that she was holding her breath or keeping one hand on the phone; if Brad Edwards had been really interested, she thought, he'd have returned her call before now. It had been forty-eight hours since she'd left a message for him.

I was right, she thought. *He had a passing fancy for the car, and now it's passed.* And of course his fickle interest—and Wyatt's interference—had cost her any hope for a nice little profit. Why had she let him stop her, anyway? She should have kept right on talking. At least she could have given it her best shot—and if it had worked there would be one less car on the lot and some extra cash in the till.

An hour later, with her head pounding despite the aspirin and her throat feeling raw—and still no telephone call—Melanie gave up.

She drove the Ford home. Then she made herself a cup of herbal tea, put on her favorite pair of flannel pajamas, drew the curtains in the living room, and settled down on the couch to watch an old movie. With any luck, it would be dull enough to put her to sleep. Scruffy was a warm, firm bolster under her knees, the cats behaved like a heating pad in her lap, and she sank into the couch cushions with a sigh of relief.

Her nose twitched. There was a half-familiar spicy scent on the pillow. Wyatt's aftershave, she concluded. She wondered, as she drifted off, what he would say if she accused him of marking territory....

She didn't know how much later it was when she woke, and in the first instant of consciousness she wasn't sure what had roused her. Then Scruffy, still lying under her bent knees, bristled and gave a low, almost hoarse growl, and she realized that what she'd heard was the click of the front door opening.

The room was dusky, but with the curtains closed she couldn't tell what time it was. Was it late enough that a burglar, prospecting for a target, would see the darkened house and assume it was empty? She was gone so much of the time— Surely she couldn't be so unlucky as to actually be at home on the one occasion when a burglar chose to pay a call. Maybe if she lay very still...

Scruffy wriggled free and bounded across the room toward the door as it slowly swung open. One of the hinges creaked a little.

The streetlights were on outside—she must have slept

for hours—and Melanie could see a figure silhouetted against the glow. A man, definitely. He was tall, broad-shouldered, and carrying something that looked like grocery bags.

She sank back with a sigh of relief. Burglars were usually burdened with packages when they left a house, not when they arrived. And besides, she recognized the shape.

Scruffy started to wag his tail and dance around the intruder, begging.

"Have you no pride, Scruff?" Melanie asked. "No dignity? Wyatt isn't always going to have a steak bone for you." She sat up straighter. "It's nice of you to stop by, but would you care to explain how you got in? Can you pick locks, along with all your other talents?"

"That would be a handy skill," Wyatt said. "I'll put it on my list of things to learn. But as a matter of fact, Robbie told me you always keep a spare key in your desk in case of emergencies."

"I don't like the sound of that," Melanie said. "What's going on at the shop that makes this an emergency?"

"Nothing. It's all under control. But I figured a mission of mercy would be better received if you didn't have to wake up, drag yourself out of bed, and come downstairs to answer the bell."

She couldn't exactly argue with that. "Well, it still wasn't too bright of you just to appropriate the key."

"I didn't steal it," Wyatt pointed out. "Robbie dug it out for me."

"It certainly didn't take you long to figure out how to get around him. But that's not what I meant. I was talking about you just walking in without even a knock. You're lucky I didn't hear you just a little earlier, or—"

"Or what? You'd have set the dog on me?" He looked down at Scruffy, who was sitting up on his haunches with one paw on Wyatt's knee, his eyes wistful. "I'm terrified."

"I'd have been standing beside the door with the rolling pin, and you'd be on the carpet right now with a very large bump on your head."

"Judging by what Robbie said about how you were feeling, you wouldn't have the strength."

"Don't underestimate me, Wyatt. I only have a cold."

"So if you're completely able-bodied, why are you sitting here in the dark? Turn on a light, will you? I'm afraid I'll trip over something and drop your care package. Or even if I manage to get it across the room safely, you might mistake the flowerpot for the soup carton and eat the tulips."

Melanie hesitated just an instant, then shrugged and reached up to turn on a lamp beside the couch. It wasn't like seeing her in pajamas was going to be any kind of a turn-on for him. Her man-styled outfit had been a long way from exotic lingerie to begin with, and it had been washed so many times that the flannel was faded almost to white. Besides, he'd seen her in pajamas before. "You brought me soup? I can't remember the last time anyone did that."

He nodded. "Chicken noodle—of course." He came across the room and set two bags down on the trunk which served as a coffee table.

Melanie watched as he unpacked the contents. There was a foam carton which smelled heavenly, a small loaf of crusty French bread, a box of chocolates, and a large pot of tulips, bursting with buds which were open just enough to reveal yellow petals tipped with red.

I prefer flowers that last, she'd said. He'd actually remembered.

He handed her a spoon and popped the lid off the soup carton. ''Dig in.''

''How did you know I was sick, anyway? From Robbie, obviously—but how? And why?''

''He called me.'' Wyatt sat down on the other end of the couch.

''To tell you I was sick? That's ridiculous.'' She took a deep breath of the steaming broth and felt nourished simply by the rich aroma. She hadn't realized she was hungry.

''No. He called me because he had a question and didn't want to bother you.''

''A question about what?'' Melanie asked warily.

''The price of the Ford. Don't worry, it's handled.''

She paused with her spoon halfway to her mouth. ''Brad Edwards called back? Damn, I knew I shouldn't have come home.''

''Don't worry about it. I talked to him, and we cut a deal. All the paperwork's signed—I left it on your desk.''

''You sold him the Ford?''

Wyatt nodded. ''He wanted it right away, but I told him we couldn't deliver it until tomorrow. That's the other reason I stopped by—so you wouldn't take off with it. Eat your soup while it's hot.''

''Wyatt, I don't remember telling you how much I wanted for the Ford.''

''You didn't,'' he said cheerfully. ''And you didn't tell Robbie either. That's why he called me—to see if I knew.''

Melanie dropped the spoon into the container and pushed it aside. All of a sudden, she'd lost her appetite.

"I pulled the file, saw what you had paid for parts, checked the log on how much labor went into it, compared the markup on a couple of other cars you've sold lately, and took a guess about what it was worth." He sounded very proud of himself.

Melanie's head was throbbing again. The pieces were starting to fit together, but she didn't like the picture they formed.

Brad Edwards had been in no hurry at all to call her back, even to begin discussing a price. Yet when he suddenly found himself dealing with Wyatt instead, he'd been in a rush not only to finish the paperwork but to get possession of his new toy. She wouldn't be surprised if he'd been eager to get his hands on the car before Melanie even found out about the deal.

That led her to an obvious—and ominous—conclusion. Brad Edwards was a businessman. For him to agree to a price so quickly, he must have felt he was getting a deal he couldn't refuse. Which meant that Wyatt must have offered him the bargain of the century. "What kind of idiotic price did you quote him, Wyatt?"

"How odd that you should call it an idiotic price," Wyatt mused.

Melanie gritted her teeth. "Why is it odd?"

"Because that's just about the same phrase Robbie used."

"I don't suppose it occurred to you to consult him until after you'd already cut the deal?" It wasn't really a question. *Men,* she fumed. *Why do they always assume they know everything?*

If he had sold that car at a giveaway level…. She *would* set Scruffy on him, Melanie decided. Not that the dog would exactly tear him limb from limb—that wasn't

Scruffy's style—but in the long run, she supposed, being licked to death would be just as effective a punishment.

Wyatt was still talking.

Melanie pulled herself back from planning his imminent demise and, using every ounce of self-control she possessed, listened to how he'd arrived at an asking price for the Ford, and what Brad had said.

Then she forced herself to swallow hard, despite the rawness in her throat, and finally she managed to speak. Her voice felt hoarse and strained. "You got ten thousand dollars more than I would have dared to ask for."

"Funny," Wyatt murmured. "That's exactly what Robbie told me you'd say."

He had brought enough soup to feed the cavalry, so the least she could do in the way of making amends was to offer to share it and the French bread, and to add a glass of wine from the bottle in her refrigerator to toast Wyatt's success in his first deal.

Melanie was almost giddy over the news. The asking price she'd had in mind for the Ford would have produced a nice profit, but Wyatt's deal was phenomenal. An extra ten thousand dollars right now would not only ease the cash flow situation but would make the business look better to prospective buyers. "When we start showing the books, that will be a very nice entry to point out."

Wyatt swirled his wine and sipped. "So you're saying I didn't do badly for a rookie, eh?"

She held up her glass in salute. "You're a natural. Are you positive you don't want to buy me out and run the business yourself?"

"Absolutely I'm sure. What are you going to do with the extra ten grand?"

She frowned. "I wasn't planning on doing anything particular with it. Well, maybe give the guys a bonus—they're the ones who did all the work."

He grinned. "And you're saying I didn't?"

"Well, you get your half of the profits to start with, so—oh, stop pulling my chain."

"I didn't start it—you did, when you suggested I might want to buy your half of the business after all."

She didn't think it would be prudent to tell him that she hadn't exactly been joking.

"They must have taken the news pretty well," Wyatt said. "It seemed pretty calm when I was there."

"The news? Oh, yes. About selling." She plucked at her napkin and didn't look at him. "I didn't tell them. Fred was late this morning, so I decided to wait till I could tell them all together. Then we got busy, and then I felt ill—and I forgot."

"You *forgot?*"

She felt miserable. "I'll do it tomorrow."

He didn't say anything for a long time. "Nobody's forcing you to sell, Melanie."

"No—I want to. Really I do."

"It doesn't sound like it sometimes." Wyatt reached for the almost-empty soup carton. "If you're finished with this, I'll clear up the debris before I go."

She nodded, and told herself it was silly to feel let down that he was leaving. He'd been very generous as it was, bringing her supper and chocolate and flowers as well as the best news she'd heard all week. Of course he wanted to get home, get on with his life...

It was the first time she realized she didn't know much of anything about his life, and before she could stop herself, the question was out. "Is someone waiting for you?"

He paused in the doorway. "Like a girlfriend, you mean?"

"I'm sorry. That sounded as if I was prying. It's none of my business."

He walked on into the kitchen, and she heard the cabinet door open and the soup carton drop into the garbage can before he came back into the living room. "Not even a dog, I'm afraid. Sorry to disappoint you."

At her feet, Scruffy gave a little sigh.

Melanie forced herself to smile. "Well, he sounds relieved that there's no one to displace him."

To her surprise, Wyatt came back to the couch and sat down, at an angle where he was almost facing her. Scruffy pushed a rope-tug toy into Wyatt's hand. "I think it's time you tell me what you want, Melanie. Sometimes you sound eager to get away from the cars, and sometimes it seems as if you don't want to sell at all."

She bit her lip. "I suppose you're right, in a way. If I knew we could get a really good price—"

"Why? What's so important about the money? What do you want to do with it? Train more companion dogs for the kids in the hospital?"

She shook her head. "No." She took a deep breath and for the first time in three years gave voice to the dream which had been silent since the day her father died. "I want to *really* help them. I want to be a doctor."

A doctor. Wyatt supposed he should have seen that one coming. Hadn't she said something yesterday about having been a volunteer at the hospital even before she'd discovered Scruffy's talents? And Erika had made some derogatory remark about Melanie grinding away at science courses when she was in college…

She obviously realized that he'd been taken by surprise, and she drew back defensively. "I know it sounds silly. What makes me think I could do it, after so long? I never really got a good start in the first place—I was only halfway through college when my father died and I had to quit. Now that I'm older, it would all be so much harder. I'd almost have to start over, and it would take years. And lots and lots of money."

"There are scholarships. Loan programs."

She shook her head. "Only brilliant students get scholarships—and they're usually not people who have been running car dealerships for a couple of years, they're the ones who have already done major research. As for loans—do you have any idea how much it would actually cost? It's not just the tuition for college and medical school, it's all the living expenses along the way. I'd be so far in debt by the time I finished I'd never work my way out."

"Unless someone comes along who wants this business badly enough to pay very well for it," Wyatt said slowly.

"That's about the size of it."

As if it hadn't been enough of a challenge to simply get a decent price out of the business, Wyatt thought, now it was a matter of finding a fortune. He might as well try to push the Ford to New York City with his nose.

"If I can't get a good price, then I'd be better off not to sell at all," Melanie went on. "As my own boss, I can keep my schedule flexible enough so I can volunteer at the hospital. At least that way I can be involved with the kids, and I feel that I'm doing some good, even if it isn't as much as I'd like." She took a deep breath. "I know I need to be sensible."

He knew it, too. He knew what an enormous challenge she'd set forth, and how very difficult it would be to make it all work. And yet, as he looked at her sitting there, tiny and defiant in her faded flannel, he couldn't bring himself to agree. He heard himself say, "We'll figure something out."

She gave a heavy, hopeless-sounding sigh. "Right."

He reached out and turned her face toward his. "I said, we'll figure something out, Melanie."

Her eyes were emerald pools, full of loss and pain and longing, and he couldn't stop himself from leaning toward her. He tipped her chin up and noticed the little flutter of her pulse at the base of her throat, where the neckline of her pajamas plunged invitingly into shadow.

"You shouldn't get too close," she said almost hoarsely.

He brushed the pad of his thumb across her lower lip. "Why? Because you don't want me to?"

"Don't be silly," she said, but her voice trembled a little. "Don't you know anything about viruses? I'm contagious."

Reluctantly, he pulled back.

But she was wrong, Wyatt thought. She was a whole lot more than just contagious. This woman was life-threatening.

CHAPTER SEVEN

MELANIE could have slapped herself. *You shouldn't get too close—I'm contagious.* Oh, that was smooth…. She might as well have just come straight out and said that if only she didn't have this nasty cold, she'd want to be kissed.

Not that she actually *did* want to be kissed, of course. What was the matter with her, anyway? Normally she didn't have any trouble saying what she meant. Or—more to the point just now—not saying what she didn't mean. But if Wyatt was of a mind to take her literally… What if he brushed aside the idea of catching her cold and kissed her anyway?

Then you get kissed, she told herself. *Why are you making such a big deal out of it?*

It certainly wasn't as if she had never been kissed before. Compared to Erika's record, Melanie's experience would look like a guppy mounted next to a marlin. But still, she was hardly a novice. She knew her way around a good-night kiss, and she'd handled her share of lovers'-lane kisses, too. She'd dated a lot in high school, a bit less frequently in college as she'd settled down to her studies, and not much at all since she'd taken over the business. But kissing was like riding a bike, she thought. It was something that you didn't ever forget how to do, even if the skills grew a little rusty.

"Oh, the hell with it," Wyatt said under his breath, and his mouth came down on hers in a soft demand.

But there was a fallacy in relying on previous expe-

rience, Melanie quickly realized. None of it applied—
because this wasn't a good-night kiss. It wasn't even a
lovers' lane kiss. It was a sonata in seduction.

That was the last coherent thought to drift through her
head for quite a while, until she became aware that
Scruffy, sitting at her feet with his rubber ring in his
mouth, had started to whine, softly at first but with in-
creasing volume and decreasing patience.

Wyatt obviously heard it, too, for he took one last
nibble at her lower lip and drew back. "I may have to
revise my opinion of the mop." He sounded a little
breathless. "It's beginning to look as if he's the only
one here who has any sense at all."

Wyatt had left in such a hurry, after that aborted kiss,
that they hadn't talked any more about the Ford. But
there was probably nothing to discuss, Melanie told herself as she drove to work the next morning. He had said
he'd left the paperwork on her desk, so he'd no doubt
also jotted down the address where Brad Edwards
wanted the Ford delivered. One of the guys could follow
her across town in order to give her a ride back. She
could even call a cab. There was no need for Wyatt to
be involved at all.

And it would be just as well if he wasn't, she thought
when she walked into the shop to say good morning,
because the first thing she saw was four very interested
faces turning instantly in her direction.

Fred almost cracked his head on the hood of the car
he was working on as he dragged himself out of the
engine to take a good look at her. It didn't take much
skill to deduce that Robbie and his guys had all known
where Wyatt was headed last night when he left the shop
with her spare key...

Which he hadn't returned, she belatedly realized. He must have automatically dropped it in his pocket as soon as he'd unlocked the door. She'd have to make a point of asking for it back—though she'd be careful to do it when they didn't have an audience.

"Good morning, everybody," she said briskly. "Mr. Barnett is planning to pick up his Model T tomorrow. Will there be any problem with having it ready to deliver?"

Robbie shook his head. "Just a little fine-tuning left to do, and a whole lot of cleanup."

"Good. Then the next one on the delivery list is Angela Dawson's Cobra. Have all the parts come in?"

"Pretty much," Robbie said. "We're still missing a few small things."

"Get me a list, will you, so I can check on them? After the Cobra I think we'll tackle that Pontiac, so we may as well pull it into the empty bay and take a look."

Fred nodded. "Want me to try to start it up?"

"For heaven's sake, no. Sorry, but you'll have to push it. Karl, as soon as it's inside, take a good look at it and then check out the far row in the yard. I think there are a couple more Pontiacs back there but I'm not sure what year they are or what shape they're in. Give Robbie an idea of what pieces we'll be able to pull off them and what we'll need to look for somewhere else."

"You got it," Karl said.

"Can you spring someone for an hour this morning, Robbie? I'm going to take the Ford over to Mr. Edwards and I'll need a ride back."

Robbie looked startled. "Wyatt said he'd come in to do that."

Melanie tried to keep her voice casual. "Well, he must have been planning ahead in case I was still off sick today. But since I'm here and feeling just fine, there's no need to wait for him.''

"Yes, ma'am," Robbie said. "Fred's tied up with the Cobra, but Karl can take off.''

That's interesting, Melanie thought. She'd been working with Robbie for the better part of three years. Wyatt had showed up just three days ago. *But he calls Wyatt by his first name, and addresses me as ma'am.*

That reminded her of her promise to Wyatt. It was time to live up to her responsibility as the boss and tell her employees what was going on. "Guys, I need to talk to you for a minute about some serious stuff. We're going to be a little unsettled for a while, here, because Wyatt and I are going to put the business up for sale. I wanted you to hear it from me rather than—''

Fred gasped. "The whole thing?''

"The whole thing.'' She looked from one shocked face to the next. This was exactly what she'd been afraid would happen—that her guys would be worried and fearful long before there was any reason for them to be concerned about the stability of their jobs. She tried to soften the blow. "Please don't panic. Nothing's going to change immediately. We haven't had an offer and we don't even have a buyer in mind at the moment. All the arrangements will take a little time, and there will be plenty of warning before there's any change.''

"So what do we do?'' Karl asked.

"We carry on just like normal.'' She smiled. "Please—for my sake. If any of you quit on me now, I'll go jump off the top of the Liberty Memorial.''

"Is all this a secret?'' Robbie asked. It was obviously part question and part caution, because he was looking at Fred as if he expected the man would rush straight out and announce the news.

Melanie was grateful for both the warning and the opportunity to head off trouble before it began. "Not exactly secret, but I'd like to keep it to ourselves as long as we can. Any change of ownership will make customers uncomfortable for a while, but if we can keep it quiet until there's a new owner ready to take over, there won't be much disruption."

"But—" Fred began.

Melanie cut across the interruption. "If they hear the news before there's a firm deal, there could be serious fallout. It might mean—for instance—that Angela Dawson would decide to take her Cobra somewhere else to finish the restoration. And then you wouldn't be able to flirt with her when she comes in to check on it, Fred."

Fred grinned sheepishly and shuffled his feet. "Okay, not a word."

The shop door opened behind Melanie and a man called, "Hey, is anybody working around this place today?"

Melanie recognized the voice. Bill Myers, no doubt shopping for another piece for his classic Mustang. Which meant, if they had it, that she'd have to take one of the men out of the shop to go strip the part...

"If you have any questions about this, guys," she said quietly, "don't stew about it. Come and talk to me. Bill, what can we do for you today? What does the Mustang need now?"

"Not a thing." He beamed. "But now that it's almost finished, my friend who's been helping me wants a car of his own to work on. It seems I got him hooked on the whole idea."

She hadn't seen the other man standing behind Bill until then, but she recognized him from previous trips. "Hi, Joe."

"So I brought him down," Bill went on. "I told him—this is the only place to go, and Melanie's the only one to deal with."

Melanie was taken aback. That was an element of the deal which she hadn't even considered before—the fact that some of her customers might feel a loyalty to her personally rather than to the business as an entity. She'd never thought of herself as an icon of the classic cars business.... But then, Bill Myers was one of a kind.

She stepped from the shop into the showroom and pulled the door closed behind her. "What are you looking for, Joe?"

"I don't quite know," he said. "What have you got?"

Melanie wanted to groan. Bill Myers and his long-winded chats were bad enough, but if she ended up killing the entire morning showing his friend every car on the lot...

A customer is a customer, she reminded herself.

"Why don't you start by wandering around out in the yard, just to see what appeals to you?" she suggested. "Then once you have a model in mind, we can get down to business and see what kind of a deal we can make."

Joe nodded. "That sounds like fun. Coming, Bill?"

"No, no. You go ahead, I'm going to talk to Melanie."

Groaning wouldn't be relief enough, Melanie decided, but a good healthy scream might help. "Maybe you should go along with him, Bill. A second opinion is always a good idea, and with all of your experience, you can help Joe choose a car that he—"

"Oh, I wouldn't want to influence him. Just because I think the Mustang's the best car ever built doesn't mean that's what he'll want. You go look around, Joe. I'll just be in Melanie's office."

He followed her, almost stepping on her heels. She could hardly keep him out, especially since the only place to sit in the showroom was the single tall stool by the packing counter. *We need to add a waiting area,* she thought, and then remembered that it wasn't going to be her problem—or her decision to make—for much longer.

"I hope you don't mind if I work while you talk," Melanie said. "I've got an awfully lot to do this morning."

"You go right ahead," Bill said. He pulled the chair up close to the end of the desk. "I just like to watch you."

Melanie thought philosophically that his preference for watching people work might well explain why Bill's Mustang still wasn't done. He'd been working on it when she'd come to work at the junkyard. In fact, to the best of her recollection, he'd been her first customer—and he'd had to patiently explain to her what the part that he needed looked like, and where to find it.

Bill leaned forward as if to study her desk. "What's the big project today?"

Melanie looked thoughtfully at him. "Actually, you could give me a hand with this one, Bill. We're trying to get all the old cars we've worked on back together. If you'd help pass the word—"

"Sure thing. I'll tell the guys down at the car club. Or better yet, we've got a meeting this Saturday night—you could come and talk to them yourself. They'd love to have you as a speaker, and if you liked the meeting, you might even want to join. I could pick you up—"

"I'm sorry, Bill, but I've made plans for Saturday evening." She turned away from him to the computer screen and pulled up the database so she could start noting addresses and phone numbers. At least she'd have a list ready whenever Wyatt figured out what kind of a reunion he had in mind.

It was a couple of minutes before she noticed that Bill had gone silent.

She looked up, watching in fascination as he swallowed hard and his Adam's apple bobbed up and down.

"It's true, then," Bill said finally. "What I heard."

Melanie was lost for a moment, unable to figure out what he meant. Surely he couldn't have heard about the plan to sell. But what other rumor might be circulating...

"This new fellow in the business. I hear he's partners with you in more than just cars." His voice was low, as if he were talking about something X-rated.

Well, you didn't expect the guys to keep a good story to themselves, did you? An overnight stay on the weekend, a key borrowed last night so he could pop in to see her... She'd better put a stop to that tale, if it wasn't already too late. "No, Bill," she said firmly. "It's just the cars. What you heard is a juicy bit of speculation, that's all."

Bill's face brightened. "Then he's not the reason you're busy on Saturday night?"

Melanie was feeling wary, but she told the truth. "No, he's not. But I have already made plans. I always—"

Bill jumped up. "Then it's not too late."

By the time Melanie could turn her chair, he was beside her, his arm around her shoulders in an awkward bear hug.

She put both hands up, and she tried to find the right words to fend him off. "Bill, I don't think you understand."

He hadn't stopped talking. "I didn't realize until he

came along, and then I thought I'd lost my chance and you'd never—''

From the doorway, Wyatt's voice, low and firm, cut across Bill's babble. ''Is this man bothering you, sweetheart?''

Sweetheart? What in heaven's name had inspired him to say that?

Not as much as you're bothering me at the moment, Melanie wanted to say. Of all the ways to make a bad situation worse...

Bill was staring at her, his brown eyes wide and reproachful. All of a sudden, she realized what he'd reminded her of, the other day when he'd stopped in and sat beside her desk all afternoon. He'd looked exactly like Scruffy did whenever she scraped a chicken bone into the garbage instead of awarding it to him.

''Excuse me a minute,'' she said to Bill, and edged past him to the office door. ''Wyatt, would you step outside with me, please?''

''Certainly, my dear.''

Melanie gritted her teeth till they were outside the building. ''Look, knock off the *my dears* and the *sweethearts,* all right? I'm perfectly capable of taking care of myself, and the last thing I need is you interfering and making things worse.''

''I could have asked him if you were up to your old tricks of seducing the customers,'' Wyatt said mildly. ''That would have been making things worse. All I did was to clarify that he'd better keep his hands off.''

She dug her fists into her hips. ''And what makes that any of your business?''

''Do you want him climbing all over you?''

She sighed. ''Of course not.''

''So what's the problem? I'm just letting Casanova in

there think that he's been out-romanced by a better man. What's your solution, Einstein? To lose a longtime customer by telling him that you'd rather date a crash-test dummy than go out with him?''

Melanie opened her mouth to argue, and then shut it again. *He may have a point,* said a little voice in the back of her brain. Why smash Bill's ego entirely? Why not let him hang on to the dream that she might have chosen him if it wasn't for Wyatt happening into her life?

And what happens when he realizes you're not dating Wyatt?

She'd deal with that when the time came, she concluded. By then, Bill's obsession might well have passed—just as Scruffy eventually forgot the chicken bones. Or the business could have sold and she wouldn't be coming into contact with him anymore.

''How did you know he's a long-term customer?'' she asked suspiciously.

''You were so absorbed with your pal that you didn't see me go by the office door on my way to the shop.''

''I wasn't absorbed with Bill,'' she objected. ''I was working on your reunion, I'll have you know.''

''Good. You can show me later what you've got done. At any rate, while I was asking Robbie to keep one eye on the showroom for a while, I got the low-down on your admirer, too.'' He checked his wristwatch. ''Come on. I told Brad we'd deliver the car this morning, and if we don't get started, it won't be morning anymore.''

The Canteen Club looked a great deal different in daylight than it had on the night they'd shown off the Ford by the front entrance. It looked, Melanie thought, exactly like a soldiers' club of the period probably had looked on the morning after a busy night. There were dirty glasses everywhere, napkins crumpled and tossed, tables pushed askew. The only thing missing seemed to be the smell of stale cigarette smoke which she thought would probably have hung heavily over the club of days gone by.

A busboy who was clearing tables in a corner of the main room jumped at the chance to leave his work for a moment. Melanie didn't blame him—the task looked overwhelming.

He went to find Brad while they waited near the entrance, and a few minutes later Brad came bustling out, rubbing his hands. "I thought you'd never get here. Let's go look it over."

Brad went over the Ford in detail from the front bumper to the back. If he hadn't been wearing yet another vintage suit, Melanie thought he'd probably have climbed underneath to inspect it.

Melanie held back a bit. "I thought you said this was a done deal," she whispered to Wyatt.

"It is. He's just admiring his own brilliance in buying it."

Eventually Brad turned around to face them. "It's exactly right," he said simply. "I can't wait to see what my regular customers have to say about this. I already told one of them, and of course he thinks I paid too much money. He said a—what did you call the engine?"

"A flat-head V-8," Wyatt said glibly.

Melanie was surprised he'd remembered.

"Yeah. He said it wasn't all that rare," Brad said.

"Your friend sounds like a man who knows his cars," Wyatt said.

Probably better than you do, Melanie thought unsympathetically. But she had to admire how he'd changed the subject around without saying a word about the Ford.

"Oh, he does," Brad said. "He wanted to know all about you, and the business. Said he'd like to talk to anybody who could turn old cars into that kind of money. I'll give you his name if you like. Come on into my office, and I'll write the check."

Wyatt's face showed only mild interest, but Melanie knew him well enough now to recognize the silvery sparkle in his eyes. He was more than interested in Brad's friend; he was excited.

She had already known, of course, that Wyatt wanted out of the business, but his reaction made it painfully clear how eager he was to strike a deal.

The knowledge left Melanie feeling dismayed, which surprised her for a moment. Surely she should be happy that he didn't want to let this drag out any more than she did. But when she thought a little longer, her unease made sense. If he was so zealous to sell, he was likely to pressure her to accept any offer that came along, even if she didn't like the terms. And then what was she going to do?

Worry about that when the time comes, she told herself. She thanked Brad and tucked the cashier's check into her back pocket.

Wyatt waited until they were outside. "So what do you think?"

Melanie ran a gentle hand across the chrome on the Ford's hood and said a silent goodbye. "Seriously? I believe you have all the makings of a used-car salesman. You're picking up the lingo very quickly, and the way you ducked out of answering that question about whether the Ford is truly rare or only collectible was worthy of the best—"

"Idiot. I was talking about the potential buyer."

"What potential buyer? I only heard Brad talking about a friend who thinks he knows a lot about cars. Maybe he does, maybe he doesn't. I don't think you should get your hopes up too quickly."

"It's worth giving him a call, though." Wyatt held the door of his car and Melanie slid in. "If he would be interested—"

"You go right ahead." She settled into the seat, which hugged her close. "This is a bit of a change from the Ford. By the way, while you're pulling out keys—you still have the spare for my house."

Wyatt patted his pocket absentmindedly. "Sorry. I must have left it in my other jacket. I'll bring it by sometime." He started the car. "Let's have lunch."

"What about work?"

"You'll be much more efficient after you have a good meal. You're getting over a cold so you need extra nourishment. And this *is* work. Take your pick of the three— I don't care which reason you choose."

Melanie dismissed the first two. "What do you mean, this is work?"

"We haven't made the arrangements yet with Felicity's, and Erika's auction is this week. Besides, we need to talk about the reunion, which you obviously can't concentrate on while Bill's hanging out beside your desk."

Melanie shot a sideways look at him. "But you assured me this morning that you'd stopped Bill in his tracks with that fancy maneuver of yours," she murmured.

"Well, I didn't give you a guarantee. The trouble is, nobody can predict what a guy might do when he's crazy enough to think he's in love."

"Right. I'm so glad you clarified that Bill is only obsessed with the idea of being in love and not actually smitten with the emotion itself. However, as long as we're on the subject of fancy maneuvers and what guys might do—"

"Yes?" Wyatt sounded curious. "What do you think he might have in mind?"

"I'm not talking about him. I mean you."

"But I don't fall in the same category."

"It never occurred to me that you might," Melanie said crisply. "The point I'm trying to make is that there will be no repetition of that kiss last night."

Wyatt didn't even hesitate. "Okay."

Melanie had taken a breath to force home the argument, to convince him that people who worked together shouldn't get involved in any way that was remotely romantic, to explain why it would be utterly stupid for them to continue down the path they had tiptoed onto last night. But Wyatt's brisk, no-nonsense agreement felt like something had blocked her throat and wouldn't let her exhale.

No, she thought. It felt more like a spear to her chest.

Which was perfectly ridiculous, because she'd wanted him to agree with her. Just not so quickly and so easily.

It seemed forever before she could manage to speak at all, and then it took effort to keep her voice from cracking. "Good. I'm glad that's understood."

"I couldn't agree more, so you can rest easy," Wyatt assured her. "I hate repeating myself. The next time I kiss you, it will be completely different."

The valet stepped into the car to park it, but as he pulled away from the curb and Wyatt took Melanie's arm, she obviously started having second thoughts. She paused on the sidewalk and said, "I'm not exactly dressed for Felicity's."

"You're fine. Once your feet are under the table, nobody will notice that you're wearing jeans." And that was a good thing, too, Wyatt thought, because otherwise every man in the place would be eyeing the trim silhouette of Melanie's backside...though since his own interest was partly caused by the contrast between last night's baggy pajamas and today's formfitting jeans, perhaps not every male in the restaurant would be quite as fascinated.

The maître d' showed them to Wyatt's favorite table. He glanced at the wine list while Melanie looked around the dining room. "This is amazing," she said. "It looks just the same as the last time I was here."

"How long has that been?"

"Ten years. It was prom night, right before I graduated from high school, and my date brought me here before we went to the dance."

"You remember it that clearly?" He pointed to an entry on the wine list and the hovering waiter nodded and trotted off.

"It was our last date," Melanie said.

"It must have been a messy breakup."

She frowned. "Why do you say that?"

"Because you sound sad. If it's still bothering you after all this time, then it must have been pretty bad."

"No, it's not that at all. It didn't shatter my heart that he never called me again. But you see, on the way home that night, his car died." She looked up at him over the top of her menu. "I have no idea what to order. What do you recommend?"

"I'm having the salmon, but I've never run across anything here that isn't good." He laid the menu aside. "What did the car dying have to do with him never calling you again? Unless—no, don't tell me. The car died very conveniently, in a remote spot, stranding you, and you slapped him when he made a pass.''

Melanie laughed.

A man at the next table stopped talking to look over at her. Wyatt wasn't surprised; she sounded like a musically-gurgling brook. It was, he thought, the first time he'd heard her really laugh.

"No, Wyatt. Remember what I told you about how guys react when a woman rescues them? That date was how I know. I had to fiddle with the engine a bit before I figured it out, but I fixed it for him.''

''The only thing that amazes me is that you were surprised he didn't ever call you again.'' Wyatt shook his head. ''Melanie, honey....''

She shrugged. ''It made perfect sense to me. I knew I'd never wear that frilly pink dress again, because it had so many ruffles and layers that it made me look like a wedding cake. So it didn't matter if I got dirt or grease on it. But his tux was rented, and if he damaged it he'd have to pay.''

The waiter brought the wine, and Wyatt sampled it and nodded approval. ''I thought you said you weren't much on cars till you got stuck with the junkyard.''

''I wasn't, really. But...'' She hesitated.

For a moment Wyatt thought she was going to tell him something important, and he almost held his breath. Which of course was a stupid reaction, because no matter what she confided, it could hardly be crucially important to him. She was a short-term, accidental business partner, that was all.

Then she smiled—a bright, meaningless smile—and said, ''Well, people pick things up here and there. Who knows where we learn it all? I think I'll have the salmon too.''

He gave the order to the waiter and sat back, toying with his wineglass and telling himself that he was nuts to be curious about why she'd avoided answering. ''Where did you pick up enough experience even to stick your head under the hood? From your dad? If he owned a junkyard—'' But somehow, even though he'd come up with the explanation himself, it wasn't good enough to satisfy him. It was too simple, and too obvious.

''He didn't get involved with the yard till later. But he used to work on cars a bit at home.''

That made more sense. ''So fiddling with cars was a way to spend time with your father.''

''I suppose so. What about you?''

Obviously she'd said just as much as she intended to. ''My father didn't work on cars,'' Wyatt said. ''He worked on paper. Lots and lots of paper. I don't think I ever saw him without a stack of—''

He felt the pressure of a hand coming to rest on his shoulder, and he turned his head to see a set of scarlet fingernails brushing the gray tweed of his jacket. Why, he wondered, did so many women think men would be attracted to claws that looked like those of a recently fed vulture?

''It's good to see you again, Wyatt,'' a low feminine voice purred. ''Where have you been hiding out lately?''

He reached up to remove her hand so he could politely stand. Her fingers tightened on his and he had to tug to free himself. ''Hello, Erika. Melanie and I were just talking about you.''

''Were you?'' she murmured. ''How interesting. And what a lucky chance to run into you. I was going to call you this afternoon.'' Her gaze flicked across the table to

Melanie. "Actually, I've been meaning to drop in and finalize your offer for the charity auction—but I haven't had any reason to go that far out in the boondocks lately. You are planning to come, aren't you, and see for yourself how your package sells?"

"Of course," Wyatt said. "We'll be there." And then he pretended that he didn't see Melanie's green eyes shooting sparks at him across the table.

CHAPTER EIGHT

MELANIE held on to her temper—but only barely—until Erika oozed away from the table a few minutes later with a final coquettish smile for Wyatt. Then the waiter came with their food, and so she had to bite her tongue a little longer yet. But finally they were left to themselves.

She ignored her salmon to focus on Wyatt. "And exactly why do you think I'll agree to have anything to do with this auction of hers?"

"Because part of this package for her charity is your gift."

"A very small part. Anyway, I'm not talking about the package—obviously I have a certain level of commitment there. I mean the auction itself."

"You heard Erika—she wants us to make the presentation to the winner. Your lunch is getting cold."

"I heard her more clearly than you did, obviously, because it was apparent to me that she'd much rather have you do it alone. Besides, why on earth would I want to go and watch while she bids for the package and then cozens you into going to dinner with her?"

"Why on earth *wouldn't* you want to go?" Wyatt asked crisply. "I expect you'd find it fun to watch your old pal try to make a fool out of me."

He had a good point, Melanie thought. Why wasn't she looking forward to a good time? It should be very amusing to watch the dance as Erika schemed and Wyatt... But what exactly was it that Wyatt was planning to do? It didn't sound as if he was eager to cooperate. "I doubt she'd try to make you look foolish."

"Not intentionally, perhaps."

"Anyway, I'd think you'd find it flattering that she wants so badly to get to know you. You're not actually thinking of playing hard to get, are you? Because that would only make her more determined."

Wyatt looked thoughtful. "Thanks for the tip."

"Well, I'm not guaranteeing how she'll react. Remember I've barely seen the woman for several years."

"That's why you should go—just to see how it all plays out." He picked up his fork. "I can't make up my mind which car we should take. The obvious choice is the one that's going to be part of the prize. But it would also be a chance to show off a different one."

"*You* can take whichever one you want."

"Now you're just being stubborn, Melanie. Unless, of course, it makes you nervous even to think about Erika going after me."

"Don't be ridiculous."

"Then you'll be going."

"I didn't agree to do anything of the—" Melanie stopped, noting the speculative way he was watching her.

Unless it makes you nervous even to think about Erika going after me…. The next time I kiss you…

It was perfectly ridiculous for Wyatt to think that she had any personal feelings about Erika's pursuit of him. It was every bit as ridiculous, in fact, as it had been for Bill Myers to think she would fall into his arms the moment he declared himself. But that was the problem with men, Melanie thought. They couldn't conceive of a woman not noticing them, and they thought if she reacted at all to something they did, it must be because she was jealous.

And as for what Wyatt had said about kissing her—there wasn't going to be a next time, of course. But obviously the less fuss she made about it all, the better. Making a big deal of it would only encourage him to think it was important to her.

So she'd go to the silly auction, and she'd enjoy the show Erika put on. However, she wasn't about to surrender without a final shot. "I just hope I can get the grease spots cleaned out of that old frilly pink prom dress," she murmured, "because it's the only thing I own that's suitable for the occasion."

Wyatt didn't miss a beat. "Don't bother about the grease spots," he said gravely. "Wear it just the way it is. That way, if something goes wrong with the car on the way, you'll already be suited up to work on it."

When the Baritsa pulled into the parking lot at the yard, Melanie opened the door and looked back at Wyatt, who hadn't shut off the engine. "You're not coming in? What if Bill's still camped in my office?"

"If you want me there, Melanie, of course I'll come in to defend you."

"Never mind. Does anyone ever get the last word in a discussion with you?" She managed it this time by closing the door before he could answer.

She glanced at the big schoolhouse clock on the showroom wall and sighed. What she'd envisioned as a simple trip across town to deliver a car had turned into a half-day operation. And though they'd made a little progress over lunch in planning the reunion and deciding which car to drive to Erika's fancy auction, the heart of her day was gone and she hadn't even checked to see if there were orders needing to be packed and shipped.

She was startled to see Angie in the showroom. "What are you doing here? Not that you're unwelcome, but—"

"I brought Robbie a sandwich, and he asked me to hold the fort till you got back so he could work on the Model T."

Guilt washed over Melanie. "I should have been here."

"Why? For heaven's sake, how long has it been since you went out for lunch? Nothing happened around here anyway except that someone came in wanting to sell an old Chevy, and he's going to stop back later this afternoon. So you didn't miss a thing, and I've had fun. Talking to an adult now and then instead of to a one-year-old is refreshing."

"I should put you on the payroll," Melanie said. "You're paying a sitter—"

"Nonsense. Luke fell asleep, so I put him down on the floor in your office for a nap. Why didn't Wyatt come in?"

"I'm sure you'll get a chance to meet him. We're planning a sort of reunion and picnic for all the customers who have—"

Angie shook her head. "I met him yesterday. I dropped in to give Robbie the checkbook, and Wyatt happened to be here."

That's just great, Melanie thought. Was there anyone in the entire Kansas City metropolitan area who hadn't been present yesterday to see Wyatt pick up the extra key to her house?

Angie shot a sly look at Melanie. "So are you feeling better today?"

"I'm still stuffy, but the worst is over. Wyatt brought some chicken soup, and that helped."

"I'll bet it did," Angie murmured. "Along with other things... How was lunch? You and Wyatt must have been having fun, for you to forget the time."

Melanie said cautiously, "We had a lot to talk about."

"A reunion, a picnic...selling the business." Angie was obviously trying to keep her voice light, but the humorous note was gone.

"Robbie told you, then. Don't worry, Angie." Even as she said it, Melanie knew how preposterous the reassurance sounded. How could Angie not worry whether her husband's job would be secure under a new owner? "I'm sorry—that sounded sappy. I just meant we'll do the best we can to get a good deal for everybody."

"I know you'll try, Melanie." But Angie didn't sound quite convinced.

The trouble was, Melanie wasn't so certain either. They could try, but no matter what a buyer agreed to do, there was no guarantee he'd keep his promises once the deal was done.

From the office came a whimper, and as Angie jumped to get her son, Melanie looked over her shoulder at the baby. On a blanket next to her desk Luke had awakened and pushed himself up on his hands and knees. But then he'd stopped, as if he didn't know where he was going or what he should do next.

He looked, Melanie thought, just about as confused as she herself felt.

Melanie was only starting to get dressed when the doorbell rang. She glanced out her bedroom window and saw the Baritsa where Wyatt had parked it at the curb, so it wouldn't block the drive where she'd left the gleaming red Cadillac convertible.

She pulled up the sash of her bedroom window and leaned out. "Use your key," she called.

There was no response, but a moment later she heard the click of the front door opening, Scruffy's short, welcoming bark, and the murmur of Wyatt's voice.

She opened her bedroom door. "Make yourself a drink or something while you wait."

"Would you like me to bring you one?"

Not coffee, that's for sure. "No, thanks, I'll be down in just a few minutes."

"Does that mean you're still trying to decide what to wear?"

She eyed the dress which was lying across her bed. How did he know she was having second thoughts? Or did he just believe that no woman could ever make up her mind? Not that Melanie had that particular problem tonight—there was only one choice, and the sooner she quit agonizing and put it on, the sooner the evening would be over.

She slid the dress over her head and settled it around her hips, then eyed herself in the mirror. It would have to do. The dress wasn't new, and though it was too classic a cut to have gone out of style, she had no doubt that Erika would recognize it for exactly what it was. But there had been no time or money for shopping, even if she'd had any desire to impress. Which she didn't.

Wyatt hadn't gotten himself a drink; he was sitting on the couch playing tug-of-war with Scruffy. He let go of the pull toy and stood up as Melanie came down the stairs. There was an appreciative gleam in his silvery eyes, but all he said was, "And here I had my heart set on the frilly pink number."

"I decided it didn't go with the red car."

"Well, this one does—and nicely." He backed off a step to survey her cocktail dress. "I'll have to watch out not to lose you against the black upholstery, though."

Even in a bathing suit, she'd never felt quite so exposed as she did in the short-sleeved, low-necked little black dress. That was odd, Melanie thought. Though it had been a long time since she wore it, she didn't remember feeling quite that way before.

"I think you can tell the difference between leather and silk," she said crisply and held out a hand, palm up. "I'd like my house key back, please. And don't tell me you don't know where it is, because you had it just a couple of minutes ago."

"Cunning woman." He dug the small brass key out of his pocket and dropped it in her hand. "You planned that, didn't you? No wonder you weren't ready when I got here."

"No, I was running late because I got held up at the shop this afternoon by a guy who wants to sell us a rusted-out old Chevy for about a million dollars."

"Is it a rare rusted-out old Chevy?"

"No such luck. He's just delusional. Some people think anything old must be worth a fortune. Actually, he was supposed to come back to talk to me a couple of days ago, but instead he popped in tonight right at closing time."

"I was surprised you weren't already waiting for me."

"Oh, sure—I'm so eager to go tonight I just couldn't wait to come home and get ready." She reached into the hall closet for a wrap.

"I know," Wyatt said dryly. "But I was tied up at the last minute too—talking to Brad Edwards's friend."

Melanie's hand stilled on a lightweight black shawl. "The guy who said he wanted to find out how to turn old cars into cash?"

"The very same one."

She pulled the shawl out of the closet, and Wyatt draped it around her shoulders. "Does it sound like he's interested in the business?"

"We'll see. I'm meeting with him tomorrow. It's going to be chilly tonight, Melanie. This scarf thing doesn't feel very warm."

"It will do. Besides, it's the only black wrap I've got, and I can't wear a beige raincoat with this dress."

"Why not, if it keeps you comfortable? In that thing, you'll get chilled and make your cold worse."

"I told you, Wyatt. Getting cold doesn't cause—"

"Yeah, and you also told me I'd catch it if I kissed you. Which I didn't."

"Maybe you just have a very strong resistance," Melanie said.

He looked thoughtful, but he didn't answer.

She congratulated herself for having once been successful at shutting him up. "Come on, Scruff."

"You're taking the dog to a charity auction?"

"Not inside. He can guard the car."

She offered Wyatt the keys, but he declined the honor and settled into the passenger seat of the Cadillac. The convertible top was up, but by the time they reached the auction site at one of Kansas City's finest hotels, Melanie was having chills. She just wasn't certain whether it was the cool air, the evening ahead of them, or the news which Wyatt had dropped which was causing her discomfort.

If Brad Edwards's friend was indeed interested in buying the business...

They'd have a better idea tomorrow, Wyatt had said. She'd try not to think about it in the meantime.

The auction was being held in the elegant grand ball-room, and the event was as elaborate as the location. There were baskets of fresh flowers and miles of ribbon draped and knotted in intricate designs from the stage and balconies overlooking the dance floor. Ice carvings highlighted the long row of tables which overflowed with finger food, and white-coated waiters were circulating with trays of champagne glasses.

Melanie looked from the display to the slickly-printed program that a sorority girl wearing a formal gown had handed her as they came in. "I sure hope all the decorations and food and drink have been donated," she muttered, "or there won't be much left for the victims of domestic violence after the expenses are covered. It's a nice way to throw a party, though—all you have to do is say it's for charity, and you can have just as good a time as the charity can afford."

Though the room was already half full of people when they arrived, Erika had obviously been keeping an eye out for Wyatt. Before the chill had gone off Melanie's champagne glass, Erika had crossed the room to greet them, flinging her arms around Wyatt's neck and planting a kiss on his cheek. "How wonderful that you came yourself!"

Melanie sipped her champagne. "This is quite a party, Erika."

"It's been *so* much work." Erika's gaze flicked over Melanie's dress.

She was probably assessing how much it had cost and how long she'd owned it, Melanie thought irritably.

"But every bit of the work is necessary," Erika went

on. "One must give people a good time, or they wouldn't show up to bid."

"I'm surprised you haven't included a dance band and a full stage show. How much do you expect to net for the charity after you've paid for all this?"

Erika's eyes narrowed. "It's impossible to say until after the bids are all in."

"Of course," Melanie agreed. "It would be." She ran an eye over the program again. On the last page, halfway down the list, was their package. It looked pretty small compared to some of the others, she thought. There were trips to Las Vegas and vacations on the Mediterranean, weeks at golf resorts, retreats to spas, and cruises in the Caribbean.

"Are you choosing what you're going to bid on?" Wyatt asked.

"I don't have much time for things like this."

"Or money, either," Erika said, not quite under her breath. "The last page is all local things. Maybe you should bid on a weekend package at one of the casinos, Melanie. Who knows? You might be able to buy it cheap and strike it lucky while you were there."

Every muscle in Melanie's body tensed, and she had to force herself to relax. "Thanks, anyway, Erika," she said levelly.

Erika gave her a slow smile and moved away to greet a group of newcomers.

"What was that all about?" Wyatt asked.

Melanie didn't look at him. "Just Erika being her usual catty self. I have a thing against gambling and she knows it." Her champagne had gone warm, and as a waiter passed by, she set the half-full glass on his tray. "Isn't that Jennifer over there? Jackson's Jennifer?"

Wyatt looked over his shoulder. "In the flesh," he said calmly.

Tonight, however, the blonde didn't seem inclined to seek Wyatt out. Perhaps, Melanie mused, Jennifer thought she'd made all the comment she needed to last weekend when she'd slapped him at The Canteen Club. "You seem to be making some progress on that front," she said. "At least she doesn't seem to have an itchy palm tonight."

The auctioneer called the crowd to attention just then, but she didn't think Wyatt would have answered anyway.

She paid attention to the bidding only in order to have something to do, until their package came up and they were called up on stage to read the description and to give the certificates to the winning bidder. "I'll read, you award," Wyatt said under his breath as he helped her up the steps onto the stage.

"Forget it," Melanie muttered back. "You're just trying to chicken out because Erika might buy you after all." She smiled pleasantly at the auctioneer and snatched the description card out of his hand before Wyatt could reach for it.

The stage lights were so bright that Melanie wondered how the auctioneer could possibly see who was bidding. "Dinner for two at Felicity's," she read, "with chauffeur service provided by Classical Cars, in a fully-restored red 1960 Cadillac convertible—that's the one with the big tail fins, folks—it's parked out front."

The auctioneer started the bidding, and Melanie stepped back from the podium to stand beside Wyatt. "Besides," she said, "after that very public hug of greeting, what more could she possibly do when she wins? Even Erika has some limits."

Wyatt looked as if he doubted it.

But between the bright lights and the speed of the action, Melanie couldn't keep track of the bidding, though she thought she caught fleeting glimpses of Erika with a hand in the air. When the hammer came down, Melanie was startled at the final price level, and even more surprised when it was a septuagenarian man with more stomach than hair who stepped onto the stage to claim his prize.

"Congratulations," she managed. "Is this for you, or did you buy it for someone else?"

"Someone like Erika?" Wyatt asked under his breath. "You never give up, do you, Melanie?"

The buyer laughed. "At that price, I'd have to be nuts to give it away. No, it's for me—and the wife." He waved vaguely at the crowd and then stuck out his hand. "I'm Phillip."

The next presenters were already coming up the steps to the stage, and Wyatt took Melanie's arm to guide her across the width of the stage to the ramp leading back down to the ballroom floor.

At the base of the ramp, Phillip stopped them to ask a question about the restaurant, and while Wyatt answered, Melanie looked around the room. Her eyes were taking a while to readjust, after the bright stage lights.

She was startled when a man standing next to her spoke. "So you're hanging out with the big shots now, Melanie. I thought you weren't interested in this sort of thing."

"Jackson?" She blinked up at him. "I didn't see you standing there."

"Yeah, if you'd seen me you probably wouldn't have come this direction."

Not true, she thought, because she wouldn't go out of

her way to avoid Jackson—though she had to admit she wouldn't seek him out, either. And she didn't feel any obligation to comment about her reasons for being there, or for donating the package. Jackson certainly hadn't troubled himself to keep her in the loop when he'd sold out, and now that he no longer owned half of the business, she didn't owe him any explanations.

She was a little curious, though, about how paranoid Jackson sounded. Of course, in her brief and infrequent encounters with him, Jackson had often sounded like the king of self-pity. This was really nothing new.

"What are you bidding on tonight?" she asked lightly. "The Caribbean, or Europe? Now that you're free of all obligations—"

"Oh, I'm free all right," Jackson said flatly. "Very, very free. I'm single and broke—you can't get much freer than that." He turned on his heel and pushed between a purple-haired matron and a young man wearing seven earrings.

Wyatt shook Phillip's hand again, then reached for Melanie's arm to guide her toward the back of the room where the crowd was thinner.

Melanie frowned a little as she trailed after him, squeezing through the crush around the stage. She was trying to remember whether, when she'd spotted Jennifer earlier this evening, Jackson had been anywhere around. She didn't think so—but she hadn't been looking for him. At any rate, it could have been just a momentary absence; people often were separated in a crowd as dense as this.

But now that she stopped to reflect on it, she realized that he hadn't been close by at The Canteen Club, either. Jennifer had jumped up from a table where she'd been sitting with a group of people. Melanie hadn't paid much attention to the woman's companions, because she'd been too startled by the suddenness of Jennifer's attack But surely if Jackson had been part of the group, he'd have caught Melanie's attention. Or even if she'd seen him only out of the corner of her eye, her subconscious would have recognized him, and then she wouldn't have been so surprised to hear that the blonde who had slapped Wyatt was Jackson's Jennifer. But she had been astonished—which indicated that he hadn't been at The Canteen Club—or at least not at Jennifer's table.

Single and broke—you can't get much freer than that Jackson had said. It sounded very much as if Jennifer had given Jackson his walking papers....

It's not your business, Melanie, she told herself. *And it's certainly not your problem.*

She paused and looked up at Wyatt. "Can we go home now?" she asked. "Or do you want to hang around a while longer and ask Erika why she didn't buy you after all?"

Melanie didn't intend to ask Wyatt in. It was late; she was worn down from her cold and from a series of long days and late nights; and she was longing to get out of panty hose and into pajamas.

Scruffy had other ideas. The instant Melanie opened the Cadillac's door, the dog leaped out—but instead of running to the front door, he took off toward the Baritsa Melanie yelled at him, but Scruffy ignored her and began pawing at the door.

"What were you saying about the mop being so well behaved that he wouldn't get out of a car until he was told to?" Wyatt said.

"You don't have a squirrel hidden in there, do you? Or a steak bone? Scruff, knock it off—if you scratch the paint, I'll deduct the cost of fixing it from your dog food allowance.''

''It's quite entertaining to listen to you trying to reason with a mop,'' Wyatt said. ''But I'd rather deal with this directly.'' He strode over to the car, grabbed the dog around the middle, and hauled him bodily to the house.

Scruffy didn't seem to object, for he twisted 'round in Wyatt's arms and tried to lick his face.

Wyatt paused on the porch. ''I hope you don't mind unlocking the door. If I hadn't had to give my key back, I'd be a gentleman and do it for you.''

''A gentleman wouldn't have had to be asked to return the key,'' Melanie pointed out. ''In fact, a gentleman wouldn't have had it in the first place. Just dump him in the kitchen. I don't know what's gotten into him.''

Wyatt carried Scruffy through the living room. ''Do you mind if I wash my hands? I don't want to go home smelling like the mop.''

She sighed. ''Go ahead. I suppose you're hoping for some coffee, too.'' She saw a red light blinking on her answering machine and pushed the button.

It was Janice, the nurse on the children's floor. Scruffy perked up at the sound of her voice, and Wyatt soaped his hands at the kitchen sink while he listened.

Melanie played the message through. ''Sorry about the coffee,'' she said. ''Come on, Scruff. We've got work to do.''

Wyatt turned off the faucet and reached for a towel. ''You're going out at this hour of the night to an inner-city hospital to take a dog to visit a sick kid?''

Melanie glared at him. ''Yes. Do you have a problem with that? Because it's really none of your—''

''You're planning to drive across town, alone, in the

middle of the night, in a car that's more than forty years old?''

"Let me remind you, Wyatt, that I'm not the one who was stranded over the weekend, and it wasn't a forty-year-old car that broke down.''

"Shush,'' he said. "Let's go.''

She was still having trouble finding her voice when Wyatt's car pulled into the almost-empty parking lot at the hospital and she began to buckle Scruffy into his harness.

"Can I help?'' Wyatt asked.

"You already have. Thanks.'' She smoothed Scruffy's coat and murmured to the dog, "Did you know Janice had called? Is that why you didn't want to go into the house?''

Wyatt rolled his eyes. "Let's just start calling him Scruffy the psychic wonder mop.''

The hospital was never quiet, but the hallways were dim and the noises were more hushed than usual. The schoolroom was empty and dark; at this hour all the children were in their beds. At the nurses' station Janice looked up from a chart. "I'm so glad you came,'' she said. "Matthew's not doing well tonight, and his parents can't get here for another few hours.''

"Why not?'' Wyatt asked.

"They live in a godforsaken little town in Kansas. There are hospitals closer to them, but none that would be as good for Matthew. But they have other kids, and obligations. And he was doing better, so they went home for a few days.''

"But they're on the way?''

Janice nodded. "It's a long drive, and Matthew needs something to hang on to in the meantime. He doesn't want the nurses, because we're always poking at him

But when I asked if there was anything which would make him feel more comfortable—'' Her voice quivered just a little. ''I'm sorry I broke up your date, though.''

''It wasn't a date,'' Melanie said. ''Which room?''

''I'll take you down.''

There were so many machines around the bed—so many tubes and wires and cables—that Melanie hesitated on the threshold. Then the child in the bed turned his head and saw them, and said, ''Scruffy.'' His voice was barely as loud as a breath.

It was the child Scruffy had gone to first on last Saturday's visit, Melanie saw—the new little boy in the wheelchair, the one who had been so scornful of the notion that petting a dog could make a sick person feel better.

Janice put Scruffy's special bench down beside the bed. The dog trotted across the room, hopping onto the bench and then up on the seat of a chair. Then he stepped carefully over the railing and onto the bed. He worked each paw cautiously down between wires and tubes, clearing out a little spot on the blanket just barely big enough to curl up in. He lay down and wiggled his nose under Matthew's hand, moving slowly but steadily until the boy's palm rested atop the dog's head.

Matthew's fingers twitched, stroking the soft coat. His eyes closed, and his strained little face relaxed.

Melanie moved a chair closer and sat down, holding the leash with a light touch. ''There's no need for you to stay,'' she told Wyatt. ''We'll be here awhile.''

''How long?''

''Scruffy will stay as long as Matthew needs him.''

''And that means you will, too.''

She nodded. ''No matter how well trained or compassionate he is, Scruffy's still a dog—so he can't be left alone with a child.''

''If I hadn't seen it,'' Wyatt said, ''I'd never have believed it.''

''Is this just a little more than you'd have expected from him?'' she asked with a tinge of irony. ''Scruffy the psychic wonder mop—''

''It's more than I would have expected from anybody.''

There was a strange note in his voice... Melanie looked up suddenly, and saw something like awe in his eyes. No one—not even the nurses who had fought to let her bring Scruffy into the hospital, not even Janice with her talk about Melanie's gift—had ever truly understood how important this was to her. Not till now.

Her heart twisted painfully, and settled into a new rhythm, a new reality. For now she knew what had been happening to her over the past few days.

Wyatt had frustrated her, but he had also fascinated. He'd infuriated her, but he was the only one who understood. He'd shaken up her settled little world—but he'd also comforted her.

And she admitted what she'd done. She had fallen in love with him.

CHAPTER NINE

SHE'D fallen in love—and that had changed everything.

It all made sense to Melanie now. The strange up-and-down feelings of the past few days. The way she'd felt annoyed every time Wyatt had showed up, but let down whenever he left. The weird sensation of being almost seasick the day that he and the cup of coffee had landed on top of her in her bed. The warmth she'd felt when he'd come to her house bringing soup when she'd felt sick. To say nothing of the way she'd reacted when he kissed her.

He'd even been right about Erika and the reasons why Melanie had warned him about the woman. She'd convinced herself that she would have warned any man about Erika—and she probably would have, because Erika was a menace. But if it had been any other man, it wouldn't have been as important to Melanie whether he believed her. She'd been so sensitive not because it was Erika—but because it was Wyatt.

This new knowledge even explained the odd hesitation she'd felt when he'd first started talking about selling the business. She'd found herself holding back—not quite willing to say that she wanted to get away from Classical Cars. The reaction had surprised her, because she would have expected that she'd greet with enthusiasm any opportunity to leave a business she hadn't wanted in the first place.

She'd rationalized it all out at the time, telling herself it was because of money. If the business didn't bring enough cash, then she couldn't pursue her dream of going to medical school, and she'd have to take another dead-end job, perhaps one with less autonomy and less flexibility. She'd almost convinced herself that it would be better to stay where she was.

But in fact, it wasn't the money which had been the true mental hangup, and it hadn't been autonomy and flexibility which were the attractions of staying in her current job. It hadn't been the business which she'd been thinking of at all. It had been Wyatt.

Even on that very first day, she had realized that selling the business would mean not ever seeing him again. In fact, she remembered thinking at the time that never running into Wyatt Reynolds again would be a major improvement in her life. But she hadn't believed it down deep, where it really counted.

In some secret corner of her brain she had realized that she wanted to know him better. She wanted him to stick around long enough for her to find out whether he was the man for her. Or maybe she had already known it....

But that was impossible, she told herself. She didn't believe in love at first sight. Interest, yes. Attraction, no question. Sexual awareness, definitely.

But not love. Love came later. Love only came with time.

She just hadn't realized how very little time it could take.

The night wore on, and Melanie tried to relax in the straight chair while staying alert enough to notice if Scruffy even twitched. The nurses came quietly in and out, checking and adjusting. A doctor appeared, looked askance at Scruffy, made his examination, and asked if they were Matthew's parents.

"No," Wyatt answered. "We're just here with the comfort team." He pointed at the dog.

The doctor started to answer and seemed to think better of it. He went out into the hall instead.

Wyatt said, "Doesn't Matthew's doctor even know his parents?"

"Of course—his main doctors do, at least. But this is a teaching hospital, and that young man is probably a second-year resident. His job is to monitor all the patients in this department and notify the senior doctor if there's any significant change."

"And that's what you want to do."

"Well—being a second-year resident isn't the height of my ambition. But it's a necessary step in the process."

She thought for a minute that Wyatt wasn't going to answer, but finally he said, "You'd do a better job of it. He's got a lot to learn." He looked directly at her, his gaze assessing. "Would you like a cup of coffee?"

"If you want an excuse to walk down the hall, sure."

"You look worn out, Melanie."

"I've actually gotten very good at relaxing in odd positions."

"Well, that's a talent that would come in handy if you pursued this idea." He went out, closing the door quietly behind him.

A talent that would come in handy if you pursued this idea.... Would... If... Pursued... The conditional twist of the words stuck out in her mind as if they'd been written in fire.

So Wyatt had doubts too. She wondered what his reasons were for questioning. Did he believe that she couldn't make it through the rigorous program? That she didn't have enough drive to succeed? That there wouldn't be money enough from selling the business to support her dream?

Or was it possible that he simply didn't want her to?

She allowed herself a brief vision of Wyatt begging her not to choose such a demanding life because it would leave no time for him. But the picture she conjured up fit so badly with reality that she couldn't even work it up into a good fantasy.

In fact, the choices she made about how to spend her life were none of Wyatt's business. Perhaps even more importantly, he wouldn't want them to be.

You may have fallen in love, Melanie, she reminded herself. *But that doesn't mean the feeling's mutual.*

He had kissed her—and he'd seemed to enjoy it. But he'd definitely had mixed feelings about it, or he wouldn't have hesitated before he kissed her. He wouldn't have made that remark afterward about Scruffy being the only one in the house who had any sense. He wouldn't have rushed away as if he'd had a swarm of bees after him.

And she couldn't fool herself that the kiss had been anything unusual for him, because a man who had no experience couldn't have kissed her into mush and come out of it himself no more affected than Wyatt had been.

She would be deluding herself if she thought his comment about her and medical school had anything to do with his own feelings. Clearly, he felt her dream was beyond her reach. But did he think she was incapable, or that the finances were impossible?

She might have asked him, but he hadn't returned yet when Matthew's parents arrived.

The child's mother gave a little shriek of horror when

she saw him, surrounded by machinery and tubes and wires. Matthew opened his eyes, and suddenly his face took on a wan, pinched look again, as if he was in pain.

Melanie couldn't blame the woman, because she'd been taken aback herself at the first sight of Matthew. Add in the love that Matthew's mother felt for her son, and perhaps a good dose of guilt for not being beside him when he'd taken a turn for the worse, and it was no wonder she was shocked.

Still, hadn't a few weeks in the hospital taught the woman to keep her emotions under control when Matthew could hear? The last thing he needed was his parents passing along their own fear.

After that initial exclamation, however, Matthew's mother seemed to pull herself together. She came over to the bedside and reached carefully for her son's hand. "Darling, we're here…" Her eyes widened. "What is that animal doing in his bed? I will not have a filthy dog next to my son when he's ill. The idea of all the germs—"

Scruffy raised his head, obviously curious about the fuss, and the mother leaped back as if she was about to be attacked. Melanie jumped up, shortening the leash and putting a hand on Scruffy's neck. No matter how solid his training was, if Scruffy felt that Matthew needed protecting, he might actually do it. As she'd explained to Wyatt, he was still a dog.

But even though she was watchful herself, she wasn't going to let this woman make disparaging statements about Scruffy. "He's not filthy, he's highly trained, he doesn't have germs, and he's been here for your son when—"

Wyatt spoke from the door. "We're happy to have helped Matthew relax until you got here. Now that we're not needed anymore, we'll let Scruffy have a well-deserved rest.'' He set two cups of coffee on the bedside table and shook hands with Matthew's father. ''Melanie, it's time to tell the mop he's off-duty.''

She snapped her fingers softly, and Scruffy tipped his head as if to argue that his job wasn't done yet. Then he worked himself out from under Matthew's hand and stepped carefully out of the bed.

Melanie leaned over the child. ''Matthew, Scruffy needs to go and rest now. But if you'd like him to come and visit again, you tell the nurses—all right?''

The child's mother sniffed.

Out in the hall, Wyatt said, ''I don't think you should count on a return invitation.''

''It's ridiculous. Some people just don't understand.''

''And they won't unless they're educated. Maybe that's where your strength really lies—in the compassionate end. Of course, you'd need to work up a more persuasive argument than you were using on Matthew's mom.''

Melanie sighed. ''I know. I'm tired, but that's no excuse. Thanks for rescuing me before I said something I would really have regretted.''

''Any time,'' he said lightly. ''I'm sorry I took so long to get back with the coffee that you didn't get to drink it, but one of the nurses hit me up to buy a raffle ticket.''

''I wish they wouldn't do that.''

He gave her a sideways look. ''Hit me up? Or sell me a raffle ticket? Oh, you did say you had a thing about gambling. What's the big deal?''

''It's the principle of the thing. Gambling is gambling. It usually starts small, but it doesn't stay that way. People are hurt, whole families are destroyed—'' She knew she sounded vehement, and she swallowed the rest of the sentence. But she knew she'd already said too much.

Wyatt was silent until they were in the car. "You're not just talking in general, are you?"

It obviously wasn't really a question, but she shook her head. "I'd be in medical school now if it wasn't for the slot machines and the blackjack table and the race-track."

"You?" He sounded horrified.

"Heavens, no." She bit her lip, but now that she was started there wasn't anything to do but go on through. "My father. I was finishing my second year of college when he died. That's when we found out that instead of leaving my mother well provided for, he'd drained every asset and every resource. He'd borrowed against his business, his life insurance, even Mother's car. It was all we could do to salvage the house."

"But the junkyard survived."

"Probably only because he'd forgotten it entirely. Mother actually didn't know it existed until later, after everything else was finished and done with. Or perhaps he still owned it only because no one would loan him anything against it. It wasn't exactly a liquid asset." She sighed. "Of course, it still isn't." She shot a tentative look at Wyatt. "What do you think Brad Edwards's friend is going to say when you talk to him tomorrow?"

"I couldn't possibly guess. But he's not the only possibility."

He's not the only possibility. Well, that was pretty clear. He was trying to keep her from getting her hopes up, which must mean Wyatt had already concluded that the man wasn't a serious buyer.

"Maybe the reunion next weekend will lead to something,'' Wyatt went on. ''Don't fret about it, Melanie. We'll get it sold, and then we'll both be free.''

Free of the business. Free of the responsibility. Free of each other.

Yesterday, Melanie would have wholeheartedly endorsed that philosophy. Even a few hours ago, she would have agreed without a second thought. But now...

Now, she admitted sadly, she wished that Wyatt didn't sound quite so eager to be done with her.

They'd set the reunion and picnic up for Saturday, when the yard was open anyway and their customers were used to coming in—especially the ones who were painstakingly and slowly doing their own renovations. They were the ones, Melanie had explained to Wyatt, who were more likely to know someone who wanted to be in the business.

And since Wyatt had given up the idea of charging an admission fee and giving the money to charity, they'd simply passed the word along that everyone who was interested in old cars was welcome to come and bring their friends. It was easier than creating an invitation list, but a nightmare when it came to ordering food. Melanie finally took her best guess as to how many people might actually show up, called in an order to the catering department of the nearest supermarket, and went back to work. It took her two days to catch up on everything that had slid behind schedule because of her head cold and the extremely late start she'd had the morning after taking Scruffy to visit Matthew at the hospital.

When she got to work on Saturday morning, the guys had already strung up flags and bunting and moved all the cars that were awaiting renovation into a neat row off to one side of the lot in order to leave room for the customers to park. Wyatt and Robbie were filling dozens of balloons with helium from a tank strapped in the back of Robbie's pickup truck.

"I just hope somebody comes," she said, "or we'll all be stuck here eating hamburgers and hot dogs for weeks."

"You're turning into a grouch," Wyatt said. He put another balloon on the helium tank and opened the valve.

She had to admit he was right. The week had been busy as well as stressful, and all the unknowns were starting to weigh on her. If she knew for certain that there was a buyer somewhere in the wings, then she could begin to make plans and to prepare her employees for the changeover—and to reconcile herself to the idea that Wyatt would soon be going out of her life. If, on the other hand, she knew for certain that there wouldn't be a buyer, then she'd stop dreaming of the impossible and settle down to work.

And enjoy having Wyatt around, without being so fearful of how long the interlude would last, a little voice in the back of her mind whispered.

Either way, she could adjust. She had, after all, adapted to worse things. It was the fact that she didn't have an inkling which way things would go that was wearing her out.

One thing she needn't have worried about, however, was whether her customers would show up. By ten in the morning, they'd started to arrive in small groups with well-polished cars, and by noon they were swapping stories and admiring each other's work from one end of the lot to the other. A number of them were wandering around the row of cars which were awaiting restoration.

If nothing else, she thought, perhaps they'd sell a car o
two today.

She was fixing herself a hamburger from the pile be
side the caterer's grill when she spotted a half-familia
face in the crowd. It took her longer than usual to place
it. In fact, she'd run through her mental list of the car:
they'd restored twice before she realized this wasn't a
customer at all. It was the man who'd bought their char
ity package at Erika's auction. Phillip, that was his name

He must have just arrived, and he was obviously per
plexed by the crowd. A moment later he spotted Melanie
and made a beeline for her.

She felt a chill run down her spine. "Oh, no," she
said. "Please tell me it isn't today that Wyatt arranged
for you to go to Felicity's. Because if it is—"

Phillip laughed merrily. "That's not till tomorrow
Noon at our house, so we can go to the Sunday buffe
lunch."

"Perhaps it's none of my business," Melanie said
"but for the extortionate amount you paid for a mea
and taxi service, are you sure you wouldn't rather have
dinner?"

He shook his head. "It's not the food we're interested
in. We want to show off that glorious car in sunligh
when everybody can see us, not hide it in the middle o
the night." He looked around with concern. "You're no
going to sell it today, are you? All these people—"

"I'll make it a point not to sell it till after you've had
your ride," Melanie assured him gravely.

He grinned. "That's all right, then. Otherwise I migh
have had to buy it myself. Mind if I go look at it?" He
seemed to take the answer for granted, which was jus
as well since Melanie was nearly speechless. "Uh—
which direction should I go?"

She pointed toward the back of the building, and he wandered off.

With a single word, she could have sold the Cadillac... Of course, it wouldn't have been ethical to sell him she was negotiating a deal when she actually wasn't. Still, it wouldn't have taken much to talk Phillip into buying something he obviously wanted anyway.

She turned back to her hamburger, but she was still thinking about the Cadillac when she glimpsed Wyatt coming toward her, working his way through the crowd, shaking hands and greeting guests. Her throat tightened at the sight.

Once, she recalled, she had thought his face was interesting—even compelling—but not handsome. She remembered thinking that he'd be no competition for Jackson in a Greek-god contest. Technically, she supposed, it was every bit as true today, though she had trouble recollecting exactly what it was about Wyatt's face that she had thought wasn't handsome. Now when she looked at him, all she could think was that he was the most delicious-looking man she'd ever seen.

Even on that first day, however, she'd been smart enough to know that *interesting* was more important and more lasting than *handsome* could ever be. And as she looked back now, it was clear that from the very beginning some deeper level of her brain had recognized that this man was unlike any other.

He hadn't spent much time at the yard in the last couple of days—in fact, he'd stopped by only a couple of times since the night he'd taken her to the hospital to visit Matthew. She'd been very careful on the few occasions when she'd seen him, trying her best to keep everything normal, to react in just the way that a business partner should.

But she couldn't help wondering if he was keeping his distance because somehow she had given herself away. When she'd been hit by that sudden, blazing realization that she'd fallen in love with him, had he been able to see it in her eyes? Had he read her mind? Had he somehow figured out that his partner wasn't thinking of business when she looked at him?

"Hey, Mel," he teased as he came up to her. "You throw a nice party."

"Thanks, Bub." She kept her tone every bit as playful as he had.

Wyatt reached for a plate, a bun, and the ketchup bottle. "There's someone coming this afternoon you should keep an eye out for. Special treatment would be a good idea."

"Who?"

"Bryant Collins."

Melanie shook her head. "Am I supposed to know this guy? What does he look like?"

"I don't know. Remember Brad Edwards's friend? He wanted to see the place in action, so I invited him to come to the picnic." Wyatt put a hamburger patty on the bun and added a slice of tomato.

Melanie said carefully, "You're telling me this is the same friend who's thinking of buying the business?"

"I don't know what he's thinking—he didn't confide in me. But he said he'd like to look the place over."

Melanie felt herself start to do a slow burn. "So you invited him to come today? Dammit, Wyatt—"

"Why not? Bub and Mel's Used Cars is certainly looking better and busier today than it has in recent memory."

He was right, of course, and yet she couldn't swallow her fury. "It didn't occur to you to warn me about this?"

"What would you have done about it? I didn't know it myself till yesterday. That wouldn't even have given you time to take down all the old calendars off the office walls, much less clean up the weeds and the last row of cars back by the fence."

"I could at least have tried to straighten the place up!"

"When? Between two and four this morning? There wasn't enough time to do anything significant."

"You could have put him off."

"And missed the chance for him to see this?" He waved a hand at the closely-parked rows of classic and exotic cars which had turned the parking lot into a rainbow-colored patchwork quilt. "All you would have managed to accomplish if I'd told you yesterday would be to drive yourself crazy about everything that should have been done before a prospective buyer came to look. So I thought it would be better not to tell you."

She couldn't argue with him. Not that she didn't want to, but it wouldn't be wise while they were surrounded by customers and guests. At least half were people she'd never seen before, and any one of them could be Brad Edwards's friend. If he was to wander by and hear this argument...

"How's Matthew doing?" Wyatt asked.

He sounded concerned but casual—as if, Melanie thought, there was nothing more to be said about the prospective buyer. She decided that later—when it was safe—she was going to give Wyatt a very large piece of her mind.

In the meantime she tried to smother her irritation. "Janice told me just this morning that he's doing better."

"No more requests for the mop to keep him company?"

"Not yet. It should be interesting to see what happens tonight, though, on our regular visit." She caught a drip of ketchup from her sandwich just before it splashed on her T-shirt. "Darn it, I didn't think I'd put so much ketchup on this." *Of course right then you were dreaming of Wyatt instead of thinking about hamburgers. You could have put arsenic sauce on it and not noticed.*

"I'm sorry to break the news, but your boyfriend seems to have consoled himself with another woman," Wyatt said.

Melanie looked around. "Bill Myers?"

"He's right over there with a blonde."

She followed the direction of his gaze. "It'll never work," she said. "That's Angela Dawson."

"What's wrong with her?"

"With her, nothing. With her car..." Melanie gave an artistic shudder. "We're restoring a Cobra for her. Bill worships his Mustang."

"Personally, I'd say they make quite a pair." Wyatt smiled.

Melanie felt her heart turn over. It simply wasn't fair that he could do this to her, she thought, with nothing more than a smile.

Beside her, a short, stocky man with a mustache said, "Are you the owner?"

"One of them." She reluctantly tore her gaze away from Wyatt. "Here's the other one. What can we do for you?"

The man with the mustache ignored her and reached for Wyatt's hand. "Then you're Reynolds. Good to meet you. I'm Bryant Collins."

Wyatt gestured toward the grill. "Would you like some food first, or shall we show you around?"

Bryant Collins shook his head. "Neither, thanks. I've been here for a couple of hours—I've already given myself the tour. Is there a place we can sit down and talk?"

Sunday was warm and sunny, and Melanie and Wyatt put the top down on the Cadillac convertible before driving across town to pick up Phillip and his wife for their lunch at Felicity's.

As she started the engine, Wyatt said, "What do you think of the offer?"

She'd known the question was coming, because it was the first quiet moment they'd had to talk since Bryant Collins had drawn them aside yesterday. The reunion had still been winding down when Melanie had left to take Scruffy on his regular hospital round last night, leaving Wyatt to deal with the stragglers.

But expecting the question didn't mean she was ready to answer it.

"I don't know." She didn't look at him. "I mean, I'm glad he wants to buy it—that's reassuring. But there's something about him…"

"Him? I thought it would be the money that bothered you."

"It does," she admitted. "It's not nearly as much as I'd hoped for. And the way he just tossed a figure on the table without even asking how much we wanted for it—"

"That means he'll pay more."

"I suppose so. It just seemed arrogant to me, to put a value on it himself without even consulting us."

"And you're worried about how the guys will get along, working for him."

"Of course I'm concerned. You don't know them as well as I do, Wyatt."

"They'll adjust."

"That sounds as if you've made up your mind." She kept her voice level. It wasn't any surprise that he wanted to accept Bryant Collins' offer—even if he held out for a higher price.

"We don't have bidders standing in line, Melanie."

He was right, of course. And it was foolish of her to reject a solid offer, even if it wasn't exactly what she wanted. Especially, she admitted, when the real problem was that she wasn't quite sure what she wanted.

But she did know one thing for certain—and that was what she didn't want. She would not even try to keep Wyatt bound to a business he disliked, because to do so would be a recipe for bitterness. So if the business had to sell, and Bryant Collins was the only buyer...

"I know," she said. "So...make the best deal you can, and I'll sign."

It felt as if she was tearing out her heart.

Wyatt didn't seem to notice. "Look at this," he said, and she realized that the entire neighborhood had come out to observe Phillip and his wife go off for lunch. Some were mowing lawns or weeding flower beds, but the majority were frankly gawking at the car as Melanie parked it in the driveway beside the middle-class house in the suburbs.

Phillip was in no hurry to get started; he was obviously enjoying being at the center of attention. "Mind if I try out the driver's seat?" he asked. "Just to sit there for a minute, I mean. I know the rules about driving—Wyatt told me."

Melanie couldn't stand it. Instead of answering, she tossed him the keys.

Wyatt's eyebrows soared. "What happened to not letting anyone loose with this car?" he asked under his breath.

"I'm not letting him loose." Melanie knew she sounded defensive. "I'm riding along. But just take a look at him."

"Yeah, he looks like a kid who's just been handed a free pass to the carnival—including the bumper car track."

"You don't have to be involved."

Wyatt shook his head. "Oh, no. This I have to see." He helped her into the back seat.

Phillip held the door for his wife and got behind the wheel. "Everybody aboard," he called. "No necking back there, now, young ones."

"You have nothing to worry about," Wyatt said easily.

Melanie bit her lip. Did he have to make it so painfully clear that he wasn't attracted to her?

"We keep a Corvette especially for lovers' lanes," Wyatt went on. "It was Melanie's idea. So much more intimate, you know." And as Phillip cautiously worked the Cadillac into traffic, Wyatt curved an arm around Melanie's shoulders.

Phillip and Phyllis insisted that Wyatt and Melanie join them for brunch. "That's just because you want to leave the car out front to draw attention," Melanie teased, and Phillip laughed and agreed.

The buffet was the biggest and most elaborate she'd ever seen, so huge that simply tasting a single bite of everything would take hours. But Melanie knew it wasn't the memory of the food that would stay with her forever. It was the knowledge that this would probably be the last time that she would share such an occasion with Wyatt.

Even before she had given her approval for the sale, Wyatt had made his decision. So with the two of them in agreement and a buyer waiting, it was only a matter of working out the details—the exact price, the conditions of sale. But she thought, from talking to Bryant Collins yesterday, that none of those things were likely to be sticking points.

So it was only a matter of time before the deal was finished and the partnership was over, and they could go their separate ways. No more charity auctions, no more nightclubs, no more lunches at Felicity's.

No more Wyatt.

She told herself not to think about that right now. She'd enjoy what she had at the moment. There would be plenty of time for regrets later.

She was in the ladies' lounge, toying with her lipstick and waiting for Phillip's wife, when the door opened and Jackson's Jennifer came in.

But she's not Jackson's Jennifer anymore, she reminded herself, and wondered once more what had happened. Perhaps just finding out that Jackson had once owned half a junkyard had been the final straw for an obvious society girl like Jennifer. But she probably hadn't known that till after he'd sold it, so why would it have been any big deal? Maybe it didn't have anything to do with Classical Cars.

Jennifer drew herself up sharply, staring at Melanie. "You're the one who's with Wyatt," she said. "I think you should know what sort of a guy he is."

I do know, Melanie wanted to say. *He's the kind who brings chicken soup to a woman when she's sick, and buys her the kind of flowers she likes instead of the sort that are easy, and steals a key so he won't have to wake her up to deliver them.*

"He's the kind who takes advantage of people," Jennifer said. "The kind who pretends to be a friend and then swoops in when they make a mistake and mops up everything they have."

"You're talking about Jackson, I assume." Melanie kept her voice level. "It sounds to me as if Jackson didn't make a mistake, he committed fraud. He didn't exactly level with Wyatt when he sold him the business, so what Jackson has to complain about now is beyond my understanding."

"Sold him the business?" Jennifer said blankly. "Jackson didn't sell Wyatt the business."

Hadn't Jackson told her anything at all about the deal? *Probably only the part that reflected well on him.*   And yet...

I'm single and broke, Jackson had told her the night of the charity auction. At that moment, Melanie had been too busy wondering what had happened between him and Jennifer even to consider the other half of the statement. Now she wondered how she'd missed it. It was all so obvious—Jennifer had dumped Jackson because he no longer had any money. But how could Jackson be broke if he'd sold his business to Wyatt?

Doubt was gnawing deep inside her. "Then how did Wyatt get it, if Jackson didn't sell?" Melanie's voice felt shaky.

"Jackson put the business up as a stake in a poker game," Jennifer said flatly. "And Wyatt walked away with it."

Wyatt's words echoed in Melanie's head. When she had suggested he go back to Jackson and void the sale because he hadn't known exactly what he was buying, he'd said, *It wasn't that kind of a deal.* And more than once he'd as much as told her that he hadn't paid Jackson's price....

The evidence had been in front of her all along, but now it all made sense. Wyatt couldn't void the sale, because there hadn't been one. He hadn't paid Jackson's price, because he'd scooped it up as part of a poker pot. He hadn't charged Jackson with fraud because to do so, he'd have to reveal his own illegal gambling...

"Phyllis," she called. "I'll wait for you outside." She didn't pause for an answer.

Wyatt was in the foyer, leaning against a wall with his arms folded across his chest. He pushed himself upright and said, a smile in his voice, "Phillip's already gone out to play with the car."

"I just had a chat with Jennifer," Melanie said. "No wonder you didn't tell me why she slapped you."

Wyatt drew a long breath, as if he was bracing himself.

Melanie didn't pause. "I think before we sell the business I have a right to know exactly how much you have invested in it. What did it take? A full house? Four of a kind?"

"Melanie—"

She cut him off, her fury building. "Or did you bluff Jackson with a pair of deuces, just for the fun of it?"

Wyatt's face was like stone, and his voice like cold steel. "I could have. That young man should stay out of poker games."

Melanie thought that Jennifer's announcement had hit her as hard as anything possibly could. But it wasn't until the last feeble hope shriveled that she realized she'd been holding desperately to the notion that Jennifer might have been wrong, that Wyatt might laugh and explain, and that everything might be all right after all.

Now she knew that nothing would ever be all right again.

CHAPTER TEN

MELANIE didn't know how she managed to stay on her feet. Sheer stubborn pride, she supposed, was all that kept her upright. Even if she could salvage nothing else from the chaos, she would hold on to her dignity. She was not going to let Wyatt guess how deeply this betrayal had stabbed her.

Being disappointed in a business partner was one thing. Acknowledging that she'd fallen in love with that business partner—only to find that he was nothing at all like she'd thought he was—was another thing entirely.

"You'll make sure that Phillip and Phyllis get home," she said. She didn't intend it to be a question, and it was clear that Wyatt didn't take it as one, for he nodded curtly. "I'll take a cab."

"Melanie—"

She stopped, but she didn't turn to face him. "I don't care to hear how you did it. It's really none of my business anyway—how you got your share."

"No, it's not," he said quietly. "So I'm not offering to explain. I told Bryant Collins I'd get back to him tomorrow. Do you still want to make a deal?"

"More than ever," she said. "Take whatever we can get. Just get it done as soon as possible." She pushed through the door.

The cab had taken her halfway across the city before she realized that she didn't have enough money in her pockets to pay the fare. She told the cabbie to take her to Classical Cars instead, so she could borrow enough from petty cash to carry her through till she could go to the bank on Monday.

She was still vibrating from the shock. How could she have been so wrong about Wyatt?

Because she hadn't wanted to recognize the signs, she admitted. But in fact, even though she hadn't wanted to acknowledge it, she had seen a resemblance between him and her father. She remembered thinking that the lack of common sense Wyatt had displayed in buying a business without quite knowing what it did reminded her of some of her father's odder deals.

Well, no wonder—because those deals of her father's had probably been negotiated over a poker table, too.

She'd always known that her father gambled. Other fathers played golf or told raucous jokes or went to church all the time; Melanie's father bet on races, on ponies, on football games. It was simply a part of him.

What she hadn't known until it was too late was how much of him the habit had consumed. It had seemed a harmless hobby, until he died and everything came crashing down around them. What had seemed to be a solid middle-class life had turned out to be no more real than a movie set, and like the false fronts of an Old West town, it had taken no more than a breeze to knock it down. She had watched her mother grow old in a matter of weeks...

When the cab stopped next to Classical Cars, Melanie was startled to see Wyatt's car in the parking lot, and it took her a moment to get her head straight and remember that Wyatt had left it there that morning when they'd picked up the Cadillac. With any luck, Phillip would be driving around Kansas City and showing off his borrowed toy for hours yet, and she'd have plenty of time to pay off the cabbie and go home before Wyatt came back to retrieve his car.

The petty cash box was buried at the back of the bottom drawer of her desk, and as she was digging it out she heard a rustle from the direction of the shop and then the creak of the door opening. Melanie froze at the sound of footsteps in the showroom.

Robbie stopped in the doorway. "Melanie? I heard someone moving around out here."

She eyed the enormous wrench he was carrying. "And you thought we had a burglar? No, just me, trying to scrape up enough to pay my cab fare."

"Cab fare? But I thought you and Wyatt were—"

"Long story, Robbie. And the meter's still ticking." She put the box back and started out to pay the cabbie.

Robbie was still lounging in the doorway when she came back inside, and for the first time, it occurred to Melanie to wonder why. "It's Sunday. What are you doing here?"

Robbie shrugged. "There's a lot to do. Yesterday was fun, but it didn't get us any further along on the Cobra or the Pontiac. And if you're going to be showing the place off to potential buyers, we'd better keep up with the workload."

"We're not going to be showing it." She caught herself. "I mean, I think it's already sold—all but doing the paperwork."

"To that guy who was poking around here yesterday?"

She tried to smile. "There must have been a hundred people poking around yesterday. Which one do you mean?"

"The one with the mustache like a walrus."

"That's the one. He said he liked what he saw."

"That covers it, then." Robbie's voice was dry. "Because he saw everything there was to see."

"There's no deal yet, but we talked about terms. He agreed to keep everybody on the staff."

The only real obstacles, Melanie reflected, had been the size of the check Bryant Collins was willing to write, and her intuitive sense that he wouldn't be easy to work for. But now, she was willing to take less money just to have the whole thing over so she didn't have to face Wyatt again. And as for her guys—

How do I know the next buyer who comes along wouldn't be even worse for them? But that didn't make her feel any easier about Bryant Collins.

Robbie seemed to hear the doubts in her voice. "Don't worry about it, Melanie. I'm sure if he buys it, the deal will work out all right. People who work on old cars are pretty much all alike, under the skin. We'll be fine."

Melanie wished she felt as certain as Robbie sounded. But then, she wasn't confident that Robbie was really convinced, either—she was pretty sure he was just trying to make them both feel better about the inevitable.

"You know," Robbie said slowly, "it was a big shock around here when Wyatt turned up."

That, Melanie thought, *is the understatement of the year.*

"We'd all kind of gotten used to Jackson not paying any attention and leaving everything to you. Wyatt's not a bad guy, though."

"We just don't know much about him." It hurt to admit, even to herself, that she had fallen in love with someone who was so completely a mystery. She didn't even know what he did, or where he lived. *South of downtown* took in a lot of territory.

"Anyway, that turned out all right. So I imagine this new guy will too."

That turned out all right.... Melanie felt her heart twist. *Not for me,* she wanted to say.

"There was something I wanted to ask you about the Pontiac," Robbie went on. "It'll just take a couple of minutes."

"I'm not in any big hurry," Melanie said, and followed him out to the shop.

A little later, with Robbie's question answered, she chose a white Corvette to drive home. That was another thing she'd have to take into account when the sale went though, she realized—she'd have to buy a car, because she would no longer have an unlimited choice to draw from. And then things like oil changes and tires and insurance wouldn't be part of the business's routine expenses. She'd be paying for all of those herself.

As she thought it through, the offer Bryant Collins had made was sounding smaller and smaller. But changing her mind now wasn't an option. She had given Wyatt the go-ahead to negotiate for her, and as long as he stuck to the deal she'd agreed to, she couldn't back out.

She'd just be very careful to read the papers before she signed anything.

She almost didn't notice, as she drove through the lot, that the Cadillac was parked neatly right next to the building, and Wyatt's car was gone. He must have come while she was back in the shop with Robbie—and perhaps he hadn't even realized that she was there.

But of course it would be no surprise to find that Wyatt hadn't wanted to talk to her any more than she wanted to talk to him.

Melanie was amused to notice that it was Bill Myers who delivered Angela Dawson to pick up her Cobra. He was driving his Mustang, though the blue driver's door hadn't yet been repainted to match the almost fire-engine red of the rest of the car. And through the open window of the showroom she could hear them arguing heatedly about the relative merits of the two brands.

Wyatt was right, Melanie thought. They do make quite a pair.

It was several seconds later before she realized she'd done it again—thought of him automatically, warmly, as if he were a friend and everything was fine between them. She wanted to kick herself.

She had thought that the longer he stayed away, the easier she would find it. Surely as the days went by, she would stop thinking about him. He'd be no more than an absent partner, as Jackson had been.

But Wyatt was anything but absent, because he was everywhere she looked. He was sitting in every car they'd driven together. He was lurking at the edge of every old calendar on the office wall. He was standing beside the coffee machine whenever she went to refill her cup.

Each time the door opened, Scruffy lifted his head and looked expectantly at the newcomer, and then drooped back into his basket again.

Melanie knew exactly how he felt.

She got the keys for the Cobra and went out to greet Angela and Bill. They'd moved on from the question of which was the better car and were discussing the relative merits of do-it-yourself versus professional restoration.

"I must say I'm on Angela's side here," Melanie said as she joined them. "Bill, you know the guys could have that Mustang of yours looking like it just came out of the showroom within a week or two. All you have to do is say the word.''

''It's the satisfaction that counts most,'' Bill said stubbornly.

Angela laughed at him and started up the Cobra's engine. ''I'll race you home,'' she offered. ''And you can have a head start while I sit here and write my check.''

From behind Melanie came a man's voice, low and full of humor. Wyatt's voice. ''Don't do it, Bill, or she'll never stop rubbing it in.''

Melanie's heart gave an odd little jolt. She turned to face him, trying to keep herself steady. It had been days since she'd seen him, but that didn't make any difference—except perhaps to make him look even more appealing.

Angela was in a hurry to be out on the road with her new toy, and so Melanie processed the paperwork at record speed. It was only a few minutes later that she put Angela's check under the chunk of Missouri limestone which served as a paperweight on her desk and turned to Wyatt, who was playing tug-of-war with Scruffy.

He stopped immediately, much to Scruffy's disgust, and closed the office door. The amusement he'd displayed as he talked to Angela was gone; the good-humored playmate had vanished. His face was chilly as he surveyed Melanie.

She sat up straighter. ''I'm assuming you're here because you have something to report about the sale.''

He sat down across from her. ''I've talked to Bryant Collins several times. He won't budge from his initial offer.''

''That's crazy. Nobody does business that way.''

"He says if we insist on conditions like keeping all the employees for at least a year, he can't afford to—"

"He said he'd keep them permanently. Now he's changing it to just a year?"

Wyatt said mildly, "If you'll let me finish, Melanie... You have to be realistic. That agreement is completely unenforceable anyway."

"Which he knows perfectly well," Melanie grumbled. She closed her eyes and rubbed her temples. She could take this offer, and have it over with. Or she could turn it down and continue this mismatched, unhappy partnership.

But they couldn't go on like this. The stress would do nothing but get worse, and she could feel in her bones— and see in Wyatt's face—the toll it was already taking. There was really no choice, and she knew it. "If there's no other buyer and he's not willing to budge, then I suppose..." Her voice trailed off. She couldn't bring herself to say it.

"There's one other possible buyer."

Melanie sat up straighter. "Why didn't you tell me that right away?"

"Because it's just about the same amount of money."

Melanie sighed. She'd been hoping for more, because she'd tried every way she could to make the numbers add up, and she didn't like the result. Her half of Bryant Collins' offer might get her through medical school. But by the time she finished school, she'd be scraping bottom—and she'd still be only halfway through her training. She couldn't live on the pittance paid to interns and residents, and there wouldn't be time for any other kind of job to fill in the cracks.

And if this new offer was no more, then she would still be in the same pickle.

"The sales price is about the same," Wyatt went on. "However, instead of paying it all up front as Bryant Collins would do, the buyer would make a one-third down payment and then pay the rest over a longer period of time."

"So what you're saying is it's really a worse deal, with the money trickling in like that."

"However, in return for the more generous time frame, we'd also get a small share of the profits."

"Having been in this business for a while," Melanie said, "I wouldn't count on there being profits. Why are you even telling me about this?"

"Because it also offers better conditions for your workers. I think we should take it."

She'd been opening her mouth to refuse, but that stopped her.

"If you disagree, I can go back to Bryant Collins and tell him there's another bidder," Wyatt said. "He might increase his offer."

Melanie pulled herself up short. "No," she said. "If this other deal is better for my guys, then that's what I want to do." Maybe if she put the house on the market and lived on canned tuna, she could make it. *I can always sell some blood,* she thought wryly.

Wyatt stood up. "I'll get the sales contract drawn up. It won't take long to go through, so you can make arrangements to start school right away if you want. You should have the first third of the money within a week."

"Who's this buyer, anyway?" Melanie asked idly. "And where did you find him?"

For a moment she thought he wasn't going to answer. "He found me," Wyatt said finally. "It's Robbie."

Melanie felt her jaw go slack. "*Robbie* has the resources to buy this place? He can't have been moonlighting to save up, because he's always here…. Oh, of course—that's why he'll need a lot of time to pay.'' As she got used to the idea, Melanie felt like dancing. "It's perfect, Wyatt. The customers trust him, the employees will be pleased—"

"You'll have a regular income, and I'll be rid of an albatross 'round my neck." He pushed his chair back into place and was gone before she could respond.

An albatross 'round his neck. She wondered for a moment if he had been talking about the business—or about her. The business, of course, she told herself drearily. He'd do anything to get rid of this business. But Melanie herself wasn't important enough to Wyatt for him to consider her a problem.

When Melanie went out to the shop to congratulate Robbie, he had his head under the hood of the Pontiac. The engine was running, she noted—which was a major step forward, since the last time they'd tried to start it, it had screeched like a banshee. It was still pretty noisy, though—she had to tap Robbie on the shoulder to get his attention.

He killed the engine and reached for a towel to wipe his hands.

"I came out to say congratulations to the new owner," Melanie said.

Robbie's hands stilled, clutching the towel. "You don't mind?"

"*Mind?* Of course not. Why would I mind?"

He shuffled his feet. "I just thought… Wyatt didn't want me to say anything to you about it, so I thought you might be upset."

Melanie frowned, remembering that odd hesitation of Wyatt's, the moment when she'd thought he wasn't going to tell her who the buyer was. But that made no sense at all. It was Robbie, for heaven's sake—not an old poker pal or a career criminal... "Why didn't he want you to tell me?"

Robbie shrugged. "Just being modest, I guess."

"About making a deal with you? I shouldn't think that would—"

"About helping me to swing it. Angie and I have always wanted to have our own business, but I never thought it would be possible. Even when I asked Wyatt about it, I thought it was a waste of time. I don't have the kind of money it takes to buy a place like this. But then when Wyatt said I could pay it off over a long time—I just couldn't believe it."

That's easy to explain, Melanie wanted to say. *He doesn't have anything invested, so whatever he gets back, no matter how little it is or how long it takes, is gravy.*

But she couldn't bring herself to wipe the worshipful look from Robbie's eyes. Not for Wyatt's sake, she told herself, but because it would hurt Robbie to discover that his hero had a flaw. If he found out that Wyatt had made that deal not for Robbie's sake but because it was coldly practical from Wyatt's point of view, Robbie would be devastated.

"Of course, he gets a third down," she murmured. "That's a pretty good chunk of change right there."

And there's no way that Robbie has that kind of money, she thought uneasily.

She knew exactly what Robbie earned, because she was the one who wrote his paychecks. She knew that Angie had quit her job when the baby was born and had been at home ever since. And she was pretty certain that neither one of them could have inherited a windfall without everyone at Classical Cars hearing about it.

So where was Robbie getting the money to make a one-third down payment on the car lot within a week?

There was only one answer, and Melanie didn't like it.

He'd do anything to get rid of this business, she had told herself just this afternoon. And she'd been right.

Robbie was shaking his head. "No, he doesn't get a big payment up front. He explained to me why you need money right away, and I think it's great, really—you going back to school. But I don't have that kind of cash. So when Wyatt offered to loan me that, too, and let me pay back everything I owe him a little at a time over the next ten years…"

That's the bit I missed, Melanie thought. *No wonder he was in such a hurry to leave, before I could put the pieces together.*

Wyatt was so anxious to get rid of the business that he was not only willing to take peanuts for it but he would wait years for the money. And he was so anxious to get rid of Melanie that he was willing to pay for the privilege.

Maybe she was more important to him than she'd thought. She must be even more of a nuisance than she'd realized, considering what it was costing him to be rid of her…

Doesn't it make you feel special, Melanie—being singled out for special treatment like that?

The office was too small to fit everyone in, so Melanie had the guys move the cream-colored Thunderbird out of the showroom and set up a table instead. Angie came in hours before the scheduled signing, her arms loaded with crepe paper and balloons, to decorate the room as if for a party.

Melanie retreated to the office and for the last time went through the motions of checking for orders, updating the records for each car that was currently under renovation, making entries in the computer ledgers. As soon as the papers were signed, this would be Angie's job. But though she'd been training her successor all week, and she was confident that Angie would do just fine, something inside Melanie insisted that she leave everything in perfect order.

So she was the last to join the group around the table. There were five of them—she and Wyatt, Robbie and Angie, and an attorney—plus baby Luke toddling around the room and entertaining himself by batting at each balloon in turn.

Melanie sat down across from Wyatt and signed in silence. It took very little time—much less than Angie had spent decorating the room—and then it was done. The three years she had spent in the car business were over, reduced to a few pieces of paper.

Robbie and Angie were hugging in the middle of the showroom. Luke, noticing that he was being left out of the embrace, tugged at his parents and babbled anxiously. The attorney gathered up his papers. Wyatt headed for the door.

Melanie intercepted him. "Can I talk to you privately, please?"

He looked reluctant.

"It'll only take a minute, Wyatt." She looked toward the office, and then realized that it wasn't hers anymore. "Outside, maybe?"

The wind was crisp as it whipped around the building, and she hadn't stopped to pick up a jacket. She shivered.

Wyatt said, "Let's sit in a car. Your choice."

The closest was the red Cadillac which had been part of the charity auction package. Melanie slid behind the wheel and then on across into the passenger seat, turning so her back was against the door.

"Have you signed up for school yet?"

She shook her head. Then she held out the check Robbie had given her just minutes before. "Here."

"What's this?"

"Your money back. You don't have to pay me off. I'm glad you arranged for Robbie to buy the business, and I'm willing to take the same terms you're getting. And don't be angry with Robbie. He didn't tell me, I figured it out for myself."

He didn't take the check. She reached across the car and tucked it over the sun visor right above his head.

"What about your schooling?" he said quietly.

"Maybe I'll go to nursing school instead—it's faster and less expensive. Or I might be able to get an actual job working with companion dogs. It doesn't matter—I can still help kids."

"That's not what you want."

"Well, I long ago learned that we don't get everything we want, so—"

"He really hurt you, didn't he?"

"My father, you mean? Yes, he did. But that is so far beside the point, Wyatt... You just don't get it, do you? Didn't it occur to you, when I told you how I felt about gambling, to tell me about the poker game?"

"No. I didn't see any reason to trash Jackson then— since he wasn't your partner anymore."

"Oh, that's rich. How about you? Didn't it occur to you that I might care how you'd got this place?"

"Why should it matter to you?"

The quiet question stopped Melanie in her tracks. If she'd been an ordinary partner, it wouldn't have mattered. It was only falling in love with him which had made this the worst thing that could happen to her...

He reached up and pulled the check from the visor. "Why won't you take this from me? Because it's tainted? It isn't, you know. I didn't win it at poker."

Melanie shook her head. "I just can't."

"Then that's it," he said.

It's over, she told herself. *You've done what you had to do. Now get out of the car and walk away.*

But she couldn't move. It was as if her brain had suddenly kicked into such high gear that her body was paralyzed. "It doesn't fit," she said suddenly. "You care too much."

Wyatt laughed, but there was no humor in the sound. "You're quite right, Melanie. I have a much bigger problem than gambling." He looked down at the check. "But you may have cured me." He folded the slip of paper into fourths and stuck it in his breast pocket. "You—and Jennifer."

Melanie was afraid to breathe.

But he didn't go on.

She said, softly, "You could have taken Bryant Collins' offer and walked away with cash, but instead you found a way for Robbie to have the business he dreamed of. You could have just sympathized with me about not being able to go to school—but instead you manufactured a whole scenario to make it possible. And you'd have kept both of those things completely secret if you could have pulled it off." She took a deep breath. "So you couldn't have watched Jackson toss his business onto the table and then taken it away from him with the turn of a card—it's not in your nature. But what did happen?'' She was asking herself, not him, and even as she said it, the answer began to take shape in her mind. ''You thought you were helping Jennifer. Didn't you?''

His eyebrow lifted a fraction, but he didn't comment.

''Tell me,'' she said firmly. ''Or I'll hunt down Jackson and Jennifer, and I'll find out what really happened in that poker game.''

''That would be a waste of time, since I wasn't even in the game.''

Melanie felt the world rock a little under her and then settle back into place, and she breathed a little more easily. *I wasn't wrong about him after all,* she thought.

He turned toward her and leaned against the car window. ''If I tell you, it goes no further,'' he warned.

She nodded, too afraid of breaking the momentum to speak.

''Jennifer's older brother is a friend of mine. He's been very worried about his little sister and the mysterious new man she's been dating. So when I saw Jackson join the high-stakes poker table at the Century Club, I kept an eye on him. He's an abysmal player, you know.''

Melanie wasn't surprised.

''When he offered to put his business up as a stake, I suggested he take a sure thing instead of a flyer and sell it to me. I figured when the hand was finally over and he saw the cards he'd been up against, he would realize he couldn't possibly have won, and he'd be grateful to have escaped with his teeth. He'd have learned a lesson, I'd have done my friend a favor, and Jennifer would find out what kind of a guy she was dating. And, incidentally, I assumed that as soon as he regained his senses, he'd tear up my check and keep his business.''

''What happened?'' she whispered.

"He tossed my check onto the table and drew a card, trying to fill an inside straight."

Melanie could see it as clearly as if she'd been in the room. "And he missed."

"Of course he missed. Have you ever tried drawing to an inside— No, of course you haven't. Sorry."

She nodded. "I have, actually. My dad taught me the rules, and how to figure the odds. So that's how you ended up owning half of Bub and Mel's Used Cars. No wonder you weren't very happy to find out we didn't deal in Lamborghinis."

"I was kicking myself that morning, yes. My Don Quixote impulse had cost me a cool two hundred thousand dollars, and all I had to show for it was a bunch of rusty Chevys and a redhead who was doing her best to make my life miserable."

It was a fair description, Melanie admitted. And it was still pretty much on target—though she wasn't actually *trying* to annoy him any more. Of course, if he was so frustrated with her, why had he gone out of his way to provide her with money to go to school? "Two hundred thousand? Is that all?"

"All?" He sounded stung. "You said yourself Jackson's share of the business wasn't worth what he wanted for it."

"Of course it wasn't—but I don't imagine Jackson would agree. I suppose that's why Jennifer insisted you hadn't bought it? Because they thought you hadn't paid enough?"

"I'm sure he'd have taken a second check if I'd offered it."

"I imagine so. What in heaven's name do you do that you can write a check for two hundred thousand dollars and have it taken as seriously as cash in a poker game? Those guys want the goods—pay or don't play.''

"After my grandfather sold the flour mills, he bought financial institutions.''

"You mean like banks? *Plural?* That figures—going straight from the riverbank to the other sort... Never mind. I suppose Jennifer thought you should either pay more or give it back, and that's why she slugged you?''

"She'd have been quite happy to have me take the hit for him.''

"You know, she's really not worth trying to rescue,'' Melanie murmured.

"Thank you,'' he said politely. "If I'd only met you first and had the benefit of your wisdom, none of this would have happened. Of course, then I wouldn't have met you at all.''

And you'd be a whole lot happier, Melanie thought. She took a deep breath. "I'm really sorry, Wyatt. I judged you without even listening.''

"And yet,'' he said, "you trusted me to make this deal.''

Her heart gave an odd flutter. She hadn't looked at it that way before, but he was right. Even when she'd thought the worst of him, it had never occurred to her that he might cheat her. Deep down inside, she had trusted him to do what was right. What would be best for her.

"Let me do this for you, Melanie,'' he said. He pulled the check from his pocket and held it out to her.

She looked at the future it represented, and slowly shook her head. "I can't,'' she said. "I can't owe you.''

"It's not a loan.''

"That's the problem.''

"I don't understand.''

"I'm not sure I can explain." *Not without telling you everything. Not without admitting I love you. Not without embarrassing myself past all redemption.* But then, what did it matter? If she saw him again at all, it would be purely accidental. So maybe it would be better if he knew the truth—because then he'd make sure there were no accidental encounters.

"You're too important to me, Wyatt," she said. "I can't put myself on the same level with Jennifer—being a charity case, needing to be rescued. Not when I want to be—more than that. So you see—"

She stopped suddenly. His eyes had gone suddenly shimmery, like sunlight on water.

She tried to swallow the lump in her throat, but it wouldn't cooperate.

"More—how?" he said softly. "Perhaps you'd like to show me." He moved closer.

Short of jumping out of the car, there was no place to retreat—and she didn't much want to, anyway. She didn't know if he pulled her toward him, or if she moved on her own, but she didn't care—suddenly she was in his arms where she'd longed to be, and he was kissing her with a tenderness that was more terrifying than force could possibly be.

When he finally stopped kissing her, he tucked her head under his chin and laid his cheek against her hair. "It was definitely good thinking not to choose a Corvette to hold this conversation in." He sounded hoarse. "Now tell me why you think I regard you as a charity case."

"Oh…Erika, for one. You seemed to think she wouldn't have bothered to steal my boyfriends."

He drew back and stared at her.

"All right," Melanie muttered. "I'm being silly, because all that was years ago and I'm grown up now. But you obviously believed that I couldn't attract anyone Erika would be interested in.''

"No, I thought that any guy who'd be susceptible to Erika wouldn't interest you enough to ever make it to boyfriend status. That's why she couldn't steal anyone from you—because if they'd be worth stealing, they wouldn't take a second look at her.''

"Oh,'' she said softly. "I didn't know—''

"That when you laugh, it makes me want to tell jokes just to hear you do it again? That when you first wake up in the morning your voice is the sexiest sound on the planet? That I may be resistant to your viruses, but I sure as hell can't resist you? Dammit, Melanie, where did you think I was going when I started out that door this afternoon?''

"I don't know. I didn't think about it.''

"I was going over to your house to wait for you, where you'd have to talk to me.'' He moved enough to dig into his pocket, and pulled out a brass key, dangling it in front of her. "There are advantages to doing favors for Robbie. He didn't have any scruples at all about stealing this from your desk.''

"I'll fire him.''

"You can't,'' he said against her lips. "You're not the boss anymore.''

"That would make it difficult,'' she admitted.

"Melanie,'' he said. "Will you marry me—and be Doctor Reynolds?''

"You don't mind? It means years of hard work, of long hours—''

"Of helping kids,'' he said. "I wouldn't have you any other way. Just make sure to keep some time in there for me.''

She did her best to look as if she was thinking it over.

"I think I can manage that. Yes, I'll—I'll marry you, Wyatt." Her voice cracked, and the words felt ticklish.

"I'll start by bringing you coffee in bed every morning," he offered.

Melanie shuddered at the thought. "Please—spare me."

"All right," he said. "I'll just stay there with you instead."

"Now that," Melanie murmured, "is a *much* better idea."

Harlequin Romance®

THE WEDDING PLANNERS

Where weddings are all in a day's work!

Have you ever wondered about the women behind the scenes, the ones who make those special days happen, the ones who help to create a memory built on love that lasts forever—who, no matter how expert they are at helping others, can't quite sort out their love lives for themselves?

Meet Tara, Skye and Riana—three sisters whose jobs consist of arranging the most perfect and romantic weddings imaginable—and read how they find themselves walking down the aisle with their very own Mr. Right…!

Don't miss the THE WEDDING PLANNERS trilogy by Australian author Darcy Maguire:

A Professional Engagement HR#3801

On sale June 2004 in Harlequin Romance®!

Plus:

The Best Man's Baby, HR#3805, on sale July 2004
A Convenient Groom, HR#3809, on sale August 2004

Available at your favorite retail outlet.

HARLEQUIN®
Live the emotion™

Visit us at www.eHarlequin.com

HRTWP

The world's bestselling romance series.

HARLEQUIN® *Presents*

Seduction and Passion Guaranteed!

OUTBACK KNIGHTS
Marriage is their mission!

From bad boys—to powerful,
passionate protectors!

Three tycoons from the Outback
rescue their brides-to-be....

**Coming soon in Harlequin Presents:
Emma Darcy's exciting new trilogy**

Meet Ric, Mitch and Johnny—once three Outback bad
boys, now rich and powerful men. But these sexy city
tycoons must return to the Outback to face a new
challenge: claiming their women as their brides!

**MAY 2004: THE OUTBACK MARRIAGE RANSOM #2391
JULY 2004: THE OUTBACK WEDDING TAKEOVER #2403
NOVEMBER 2004: THE OUTBACK BRIDAL RESCUE #2427**

**"Emma Darcy delivers a spicy love story...
a fiery conflict and a hot sensuality."
—*Romantic Times***

Available wherever Harlequin books are sold.

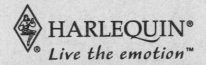

HARLEQUIN®
Live the emotion™

Visit us at www.eHarlequin.com

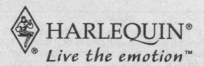

"Joanna Wayne weaves together a romance and suspense
with pulse-pounding results!"
—*New York Times* bestselling author Tess Gerritsen

National bestselling author

JOANNA WAYNE

Alligator Moon

Determined to find his brother's killer, John Robicheaux finds
himself entangled with investigative reporter Callie Havelin.
Together they must shadow the sinister killer slithering in the
murky waters—before they are consumed by the darkness....

A riveting tale that shouldn't be missed!

Coming in June 2004.